Broken,

But Not Beaten,

So Can You

Amanda Onwuka

ISBN: 978-1-7356751-1-4

This book is a work of fiction. All characters, names, incidents, organizations, and dialogues herein are the natural product of the author's imagination. Every opinion expressed in the book is solely that of the author. The responses are structured exclusively from biblical laws and principles as well as from the author's cultural and traditional beliefs.

All Scripture quotations are from the Holy Bible, New International Version, NIV, Copyright 1973, 1978, 1984 by Biblical, Inc. Used worldwide.

Jesus Calling, Enjoying Peace in His Presence for Every Day of the Year Devotional Journal by Sarah Young; 2013.

Michelle D Rayford: https://michelledrayford.com/tag/books-2/

Second Edition of this book referenced teaching and exhortation on self-esteem by Apostle (Dr.) Patience Oti. The author highlighted the understandings that Amoris's journey and trials pulled from nuggets and exhortations learned. The author hopes that as

Amoris drew much courage from the teachings and broke out an overcomer, others might benefit in like manner.

ACKNOWLEDGMENT

I thank the Almighty God, who miraculously used his heavenly-assigned Angels on Assignment and Destiny helpers to bring this imaginative book to reality.

I am especially grateful to my late husband, Charles Chukwuemeka Onwuka. He inspired and encouraged me insisting that I should cap my educational career with a doctorate degree. I count my blessings daily as I thank God for the four beautiful children with whom He blessed us: Chino, Amaka, Buchi, and Ifeoma. These children support and assist me with the difficulties I encounter with technology meltdown, while writing this book. They provided me with a new laptop to ensure that this creative project was completed without hitches. They also gave me especially useful suggestions on how the work could appeal to the younger audience by including and portraying their perspectives in the storyline. Their input helped me decide on the title of the book. I have watched them blossom into adulthood, pursue their academic and professional lives successfully, and settle down in satisfying jobs with little or no guidance from me. Meanwhile I have expended myself on exploring the plot for this book. These children were, and continue to be, my human and emotional pillars in my life as a widow. When the shocking event occurred, they all put aside their difficulties and grief and made sure I was okay. Thank you so much, Chino, Amaka, Buchi, and Ifeoma. I sincerely appreciate you all and I thank God for what you have become.

I give a big "Thank you" to my mother who raised me, Dr. Ifeoma Joy Nwosu Lo-Bamijoko; you are a unique angel from God. I thank you very much. I am sure that had it not been for your role in my life, I would not have been educated. I appreciate the numerous sacrifices you made for me. The result of those sacrifices equipped me with the knowledge and academic ability to write this book. Thank you for editing and proofreading this book. Your encouragement and support in all I do will never be taken for granted. May my God bless and reward you and keep you safe always. I can never thank you enough, Mama Joy.

I thank my spiritual mother, Apostle (Dr.) Patience Oti. for generously sharing the hidden treasures in the word of God with all who cared to listen. From the numerous exhortations you gave on the Tribe line, I learned the power of sowing seed, power of testimony, praising God, fasting, praying, and believing God. I also tapped much inspiration from the energy in the spoken words that you shared during your exhortations and I was able to write this book. Thank you very much.

I thank you, Zenaida Garcia, my spiritual shepherd from the BLD community. I believe that writing this book came through faster partly because of your persistence. Thank you for being the first to read and edit the book giving me your honest guidance, support and suggestions. Thank you, Tita Zenaida Garcia, the practical attributes I gathered from you was invested in the imaginations and structure of this fictitious book. I continue to thank

God for placing you like a destiny helper in my life; I appreciate your insistent encouragement and statement that you cannot wait to read my finished book.

To Dr. Chinedu Okoye, thank you for conducting the first professional and thorough editing of this work; I appreciate your patience and encouragement.

Thank you so much to MA. TRINITAS FARRALES-CANLAS and MILDREDDE VERA with Trinitas Publishing, Inc. For your excellent and final editing of this book which can not be understated. I greatly appreciate your suggested ideas, book layout and titles which enhanced the completion of this book. May God bless you both for your input in making the production of this book a reality.

Thank you Evangelist Joy Osueke Rolle, the woman of God who daily shares inspirational nuggets on the Tribe Prayer line. Those nuggets provided me with excellent support that I needed to write this book. I say thank you.

Thank you to my sister from heaven, Mrs. Eva Ezike and her husband Mr. Gregory Ezike. They provided me with much needed support and encouragement to write the book. They also supplied relational ideas and suggestions which I explored and used in completing the work. May God bless you. I thank you Minister Trudy Rose -Harte for your unique contribution to the coming alive of this book. Minister Trudy-Harte had recorded my testimony at a conference and sent her recording to me urging me to start the book with the recording. I did exactly that. Her action was a powerful booster pump to the reality of Broken, but not beaten. My gratitude also goes to all friends and well-wishers who in their different ways provided support and encouragement. I thank you all.

Dedication

I dedicate this book to my deceased husband, my biggest cheerleader, and my rock, Emy my love, I will always cherish the strength you built in me to face life squarely. Though there is a deep vacuum in my heart with you gone, for once the curtain is drawn; the loneliness I feel is unimaginable. I miss you dearly, but I know that God's plan for us is that we will meet again at his appointed time, to part no more in Jesus's name, amen.

About the Author

Dr. Amanda Lorraine Nwosu Onwuka, JP, earned her doctorate in Education from The Graduate Theological Foundation (GTF) Indiana USA. She holds a Master of Arts degree in Special Education as well as a second Master's in Educational Leadership and Principalship, both from Jersey City State University, in New Jersey. She earned her Bachelor of Science (Education and Mathematics) from the University of Lagos in Nigeria. She is an educator with the Newark Public School district in New Jersey where she currently teaches Special Education mathematics at Malcolm X Shabazz High School, Newark. An ardent supporter of an increased understanding and enjoyment of mathematics by all students that she encounters, Dr. Amanda Onwuka is active in the school leadership movement and liaises between school and communities in matters relating to safety and awareness. Dr. Nwosu Onwuka also worked with the Administration for Children Services in New York City (ACS) as a child protective caseworker. She is an ordained minister of the word in the workplace and graduate of Shekina Bible School from where she was commissioned for Missionary work.

Dr. Amanda Onwuka was married to Late Sir Charles Emeka Onwuka and has four wonderful children and two adorable grandchildren.

Preface

I believe that a person's gift makes a way for him or her. It is indeed our fears and shadows that limit us from being all that God has created us to be Illusions from our past often hold us down chaining us in our self-created prisons. Many factors helped me to grow and be what I am today; I thank the Almighty God who positioned milestones on the journey of my life. Reading and studying the Word of God with the TRIBE online prayer and bible group and also participating in the Bukas Loob SA Diyos (BLD) Catholic Charismatic community with the Solo Parent class (SP20) within the BLD community profoundly instilled in me the concept of praise and worship in good times and in bad. My relationship with the Women of Purpose prayer group taught me the power of intercession. Reading Sarah Young's influential devotional journal, Jesus Calling, left a lasting imprint in my heart. She stated powerfully that anyone who thought they could live a trial-free or error-free life was symptomatic of pride. For all human beings, failures are sources of blessings; they are ways of humbling oneself and developing empathy for others in their weaknesses.

In *Broken, But not Beaten*, the main character, Amoris, narrates the story of her life journey. This fictional narrative solidifies the fact that the journey through life, unless people embrace every problem and difficulties that they encounter along the way, they will have trouble transforming into what God has planned for their survival. As soon as we realize that trials and problems of life are divinely designed by God to grow us, then we can actualize our life's potentials. Think about that! After I connected with all the God-fearing groups I mentioned earlier, I was exposed and empowered with the belief and faith that I can really be all that God called me to be.

This life journey of Amoris is an imaginative yet inspired insight into the issues of many lives, put together through the mercies of God. I believe that God ordained and inspired my imagination with these storylines to empower others. I pray that this fictitious inspirational book will help lots of people overcome their fears and lift their spirits by directing them towards a positive way to break out of their feeling of hopelessness. Often, the trials we face in life break us into pieces; only those who pick up and move on are heroes of this book. I deliberately entitled this book,

"Broken But not Beaten" to challenge all who read it saying, 'so can you.' It is my sincere belief that people are blessings to others when they share what builds strength in others. The bible instructions that I received from the online prayer line taught me the deeper meaning of obeying the principles behind any promise I ask God to fulfill in my life. These teachings helped sharpen my insight and spur my determination to share them. I truly praise and thank God for his mercies. I would like to regard this book as a channel and platform of ministering to all who read and assimilate its contents. Such readers

should view its message as a perspective to share with others the hidden treasures that could be beneficial to the lives of others.

Broken, but not Beaten, in a nutshell, a fictitious story inspired by the author's belief in the saying that a life of selfishness is lived to suit oneself only. The author believes that life that does not give self to help others is a life that settles for less. In summary, Amoris tells the story of her life: a life that was full of misery, turmoil: a life replete with varied and diverse kinds of wilderness. Yet, she concludes her story in a triumphant victory. Her breakout and breakthrough came through praising God, through her seeing and recognizing the hand of God through all her experiences. She describes the obstacles her mother Amelia had gone through to give birth to her and how her life was meant to be the fresh light of hope to her family. Ironically, as soon as that light was about to glow and brighten the darkness of her background, her mother's life ended. In Broken, But not beaten, Amoris retells how her mother died in a foreign land and her remains were buried in that foreign land never to be seen again by the parents who smuggled her out of her native country, to save her from an abusive husband. In this fictional narrative, Amoris, the key character, continues to describe the dramatic scene of her mother Amelia running away from an abusive domestic relationship that would invariably lead to her death. Yet, the very escape route chosen by her family landed her in the same tragedy that her family was trying to avoid. The mystery of this episode is that her mother's, Amelia's death was not the end of the story. Rather, her death marked the beginning chapter in Amoris's life experience. God has a purpose for every breath he creates. One might surmise that God's purpose in creating Amoris was to give hope to the family that had just lost their daughter. To many, her life's story might represent many things according to their loss and belief. To others, the saying that: "a bird sitting on an iroko tree is never afraid of the branch breaking because its trust is not in the branch upon which it perches but on its own wings" makes more sense. Amoris could have told her story in many ways. Even now, she wonders how her life would have turned out if the nuns at Petite Sisters Convent in Dundee, Scotland had taken the short but easy route of putting her in an orphanage home instead of the arduous search for a close relative. She wonders how she would have turned out if someone else besides Aunty Amara had raised her. In Broken But not Beaten, Amoris recognizes the fact that no matter one's brokenness, if one persists in the knowledge that God has a purpose for every life He creates, one will break out of that situation and become a blessing too. She had learned that the becoming of any set vision is in the pursuit, in one's preparedness to set on fire anything that stands on one's way and breakout to reach one's desired height. She narrates how she broke out of her desert life. Her message is that anyone else can break out too from similar situations. From the numerous bible classes and nuggets Amoris sat through she learned valuable lessons on how she could break out of all her life challenges. One of her favorite nuggets advises people to "Garbage their past hurts, for the past is a wastepaper. Confront their present hurt, knowing that they are not alone." Amoris asks her readers to embrace their life encounters boldly and fearlessly because one can only enjoy victory if they believe they can. Once people believe they can, they behave their belief by acting on it. That is how they become who they want to be. Proverbs 18: 1 state, "Any man who isolates himself seeks his own desires and rages against wise judgment." Broken but not Beaten strictly portrays how one who isolates self can make many and diverse judgments that are unreal. Consequently, the individual creates a ripple effect of problems among loved ones. The author concludes that the most important message of this book is that one is never alone in any situation of life. So, break out; you are not alone. Amoris broke out and so can you

ENDORSEMENTS

ENDORSEMENT # 1

In *Broken, But Not Beaten, So Can You*, Dr. Amanda Lorraine Nwosu Onwuka, JP powerfully portrays the journey of Amoris whose mother died soon after she was born. The threads of this fictional narrative are so intricately woven that the reader cannot exhale until the last word of the narrative. The author invites the reader to journey with Amoris through her lonely, helpless, and emotionally draining life. Her journey is compounded by the failure or perhaps refusal of the major witnesses of the events of her early life to answer her persistent questions of who she was. If her mother died after her birth, why was her father missing in action? Unknowing to the author, she has written a book of value to medical, social welfare, educational, religious professionals, and every adult whose sensitivities she awakens to take more than a cursory look at that child or young adult seated across the table from them. These professionals meet Amoris everyday of their lives, once they identify Amoris, they should do something practical. The author concludes that one can find lasting solutions to life's challenges in one source only - GOD.

Dr. Chinedu Christie Nnamah Okoye, JP
Retired Educator, New Jersey, USA

ENDORSEMENT #2

I have known Dr. Amanda Onwuka for over two decades, but I did not know that all this was in her. I am super impressed by this work and will recommend it highly to every human being to read. Have I ever been so moved by fiction? I can honestly say no. I could not put the manuscript down until I finished it. In these days of "Trauma Informed Care", this book makes such sense that every caregiver should read it. Childhood trauma does not go away. It forms a special lens through which the individual looks at things even as an adult. Society should address more importantly what happened to a child rather than what the child happened to do. This book opens our eyes to experiences that could affect one's mental health. Let us work on developing well balanced children, not broken ones. *Broken, but not beaten, so can you*---shows a way of escape. No matter the hand that life deals you, when you embrace the God of heaven, you will discover hope and confidence. Your self-esteem will rise, and you will fulfill your life purpose. Join Amoris, walk her path and resolve to pick up some vital lessons from this book.

Apostle Dr. Patience Ogechi Oti
Senior Pastor New Jersey Tabernacle,
Shekina House of Worship, Maryland International Tabernacle,
President Shekina Charities and

Assistant Vice President of WIN.

ENDORSEMENT # 3

This book inspires meaningful discussion meant to bridge the experiences of different

generations within the same culture. It is an important message that is encouraging to

those who feel they are alone.

Dr. Amaka L Awoniyi, MD.
Hospitalist, Internal Medicine
Marietta GA - WellStar HealthCare4PPL.

ENDORSEMENT: # 4

Broken but not beaten takes you on a powerful read that is not for the faint of heart. The

life journey of Amoris is at times harrowing, lonely, traumatizing but never defeating.

The sweep of this tale brings the reader on many highs and lows but ultimately it is a tale

of renewal and hope. No matter where in the world you are or how different your life

might feel, the author enables you to connect with the protagonist and experience a

worldwide connection of encouragement and renewal. It is ultimately a human story of

survival and grit.

Margaret O'Donoghue, LCSW, Ph.D.
Social worker and therapist, NJ.

ENDORSEMENT # 5

Only the one who lived a life can tell the story of that life. What the people around you see, may not be what is happening inside you. But until you tell your story no one will really know who you are.

This is the story of Amoris. It is the story of children all over the world who have lost their parents and have had to live their lives moving from one home to another. A situation that can traumatize a child. Only a child in this situation knows the pain, the hurt, the feeling of abandonment, and the lack of love. To worsen it all, the lack of awareness of the grownups around such a child, who fail to see the hurt in the face of the child, or who are the cause of such hurt.

In the midst of all this, Amoris found God. With this, her life turns around for good. She gradually and with determination begins to reclaim her life. She feels strong and she marches on. Amoris is a winner and she exhorts the orphans of this world never to give up, that God loves them all. I recommend this book.

Dr. Joy Nwosu Lo-Bamijoko
Author:
Mirror of Our Lives: Voices of Four Igbo Women
Legend of the Walking Dead: Igbo Mythologies
Pregnant Future: No One Knows What Tomorrow Will Bring
The Vagaries of Life

The Visit
The Agent of Death
Not Again, Grandma!

ENDORSEMENT # 6

A Fantastic, Touching & Encouraging book that cuts across countries and Cultures, by Amoris whom I prefer to call "DESTINY CHILD/ LADY" A book I read with great emotions. How little we know where God's grace will lead us!" As one reads this book, you come across God's Miracles and Blessings, strong Faith too! The CHRISTIAN life Amoris has chosen to live is a Continuation and completion of the life of Christ in us. We should like Amoris continue Christ life and his works laboring & suffering in a holy & divine manner in the Spirit of Jesus. Holiness is visible in many ways with one common quality: concern for the need of others e.g. abused kids, the depressed, and the poor. Amoris has all this talents of Care& blessed with a beautiful & God fearing family. Deo gratias.

Mrs. Josephine Udekwu (SRN. NRM. RMN. RNT)

ENDORSEMENT # 7

The book *Broken But Not Beaten* is rich in content about life not only as lived by Amoris, the main character, but by the many children whose lives she touched as an educator and as a child protective service social worker. The character's own life experiences had shaped her to become highly sensitive to the unexpressed burdens of children that she came to teach and serve.

MA. TRINITAS FARRALES-CANLAS, Academic Publisher & Author, Educator-School Owner, Organizational Development Practitioner-Entrepreneur, former Trainer & Consultant

ENDORSEMENT # 8

This book has a highly inspirational and instructive content. The plot unfolding from point to point is packed with moving emotions naturally stimulated by realistic portrayals of painful experiences in life faced by certain people who might have been handpicked by God for future special roles to play in the service of humanity for God's own purposes. As a reader discovers the depths of pains felt by the central character (Amoris), one part of the book provides a glimpse of possibly deeper hurts like the brother-and-sister characters battered by a step mom and a two-year-old girl sexually abused who languished in a hospital. Such tragic experiences of some characters falling prey to life's hardships and fellow human being's bestiality will make readers suffering from life's challenges realize that theirs is not the worst situation after all. What's more, throughout the story, starting from the second half of the book, the ways to beat the harshest challenges of life are pointed out in stages, from ways to develop self-esteem to the highest – the highest being God's way. Discover THIS way in Amanda's book. God indeed makes a way where there seems to be no way, and God's timing is always perfect.

MILDRED DE VERA, also known as Millie Vera in her career as author-journalist, Editor-in-Chief of Trinitas Publishing Inc. and textbook author/fiction and nonfiction author-editor, speech writer

ENDORSEMENT # 9

The writing of this book heralds a triumph at the end of the author's training towards

transforming her life into one befitting of a life offered to God. Her own travails in life

and some confusions engendered by initial misinterpretations on the way the hand of God

moves, given how certain episodes of her personal life had unfolded, added richness and

veracity to how she was able to flesh out the plot she had conceived for the book. Thus,

her being in a position to share vital truths about how God's hand works gives this book a

special touch that can help readers understand their own trials in life. Indeed, as quoted

from the Bible in one part of the book, "God's ways are not man's ways."

ZENAIDA C. GARCIA, the Author's "Spiritual Shepherd", Pastoral Liaison Coordinator-Mission Apostolate BLD (Bukas Loob sa Diyos) Covenant Community (Rahway, New Jersey, USA), Retired Research Teaching Specialist, University of Medicine and Dentistry, (New Jersey, USA), Former Chemist-Researcher, International Rice Research Institute (Philippines)

ENDORSEMENT # 10

Amoris is a Child of LOVE! Your book is a window to another Culture. A web of

adventure and reflections, hard to put down once you start reading. Your mother knows

why she named you AMORIS! Your life is a journey of love, a profile of Faith and

courage. You were a bearer of Love. You were moved from one family to another to

bring them hope and love. "I was not blessed unless I became a Blessing to others" You

were meant to know the BEATITUDES by heart. Beatitudes molded you and guided you.

A lot of Words of Wisdom and life Lessons learned from this book. "Those who fear God lack nothing and exercise patience" As you said, the book shows Gods love, hidden deep in all the trials that one goes through, everyone is Worth Gods Love. This book is a realization that each person is unique, deserve to be Loved; is loved by God. Jeremiah1:5 Amanda you are an inspiration & strength to your children /Students It's a book I recommend to teenagers, young adults of all ages. I can't wait for a copy of my own.

I thank you Amanda for sharing, I thank the Lord for your being a part of our class. Know that you are loved by God and you are a Blessing to us SPE20
Good Luck, God Bless You

Mat & Precy Yap
Solo Parents 20 (Class Shepherds)

ENDORSEMENT # 11

Broken but not Beaten so can you is a book that can only be inspired by an overcomer. The author is a prolific writer who has proven through her story that no matter what life throws at you; with God on your side you can overcome it all and will impact your generation for good.

Evangelist Joy Osueke Rolle
MINISTRY OF CARE
Houston Texas- USA

Table of Contents

Chapter 15: Broke Out an Overcomer

CHAPTER I

Birth in a Convent

Amoris narrated her birth story as told to her by her Aunty Jackie. It was 2:00 a.m. on a rainy morning she hurried out of her room, wobbling to the bathroom, a habit she does hourly since she hit the 7th month of her first pregnancy with twins. Aunty Jackie said that she halted, gazed at her best friend Amelia, who was sitting at the dining table, with arm folded, hot tears running down her face like raindrops dripping outside.

Why are you up at this hour of the night? Worst, though, why are you crying, Amelia? She gazed with a blank, frowned face at Jackie and said nothing. Aunty Jackie stated that she ran into the bathroom and eased herself. Once out of the restroom, she sat quietly at the table next to Amelia while she reflected on the best words to use.

She allowed her some time and stated: you know you need every rest you can get in this final trimester of your pregnancy, Amelia? Remember that your baby senses every emotion you have; sitting here crying is not the feeling you want to share with that baby.

She continued to address her and asked her again. What is the matter with you? If you will not speak to me, why did you give my name as your contact at the home where you live? With that, Amelia broke her silence, saying, Jackie, what will become of this baby and I alone in this strange forsaken land? How could I have allowed myself to be in this predicament while millions of miles away? See, my case of an abusive husband has turned my life into the life of running from the frying pan into the fire? What do you think is happening to my two children I left behind back in Nigeria? What good is anything around me now? I feel so hopeless, Jackie.

Aunty Jackie narrated that she became steadfast in addressing Amelia and she pleaded to her to listen for they have been through these same questions time and time again. Aunty Jackie said that she asked Amelia to imagine how she felt when she got that call from Mother Superior, Sister Maria, from Little Sister's home in Dundee requesting for them to pick her up immediately. She said that she told her that if Ben, her husband, was not on break and came for her, what then? She said that she redirected Amelia's attention to look at her, seven months pregnant with tummy almost touching the ground, as she, Aunty Jackie, wobbles around sick as a dog, restricted on bed rest, and yet she is still moving on. She encouraged her to pull herself together and focus on staying healthy for her baby's sake. Aunty Jackie stated that at that point, it jolted Amelia out of her deep thought, and she said to her, you are right, Jackie; sometimes, I get drowned in my thoughts. I really do not know when tears start flowing out; she apologized by saying, I am so sorry Jackie. I will be mindful to catch myself in quality time, not to set off another false alarm like this again.

Aunty Jackie requested that Amelia go back to bed and assured her she was glad they contacted them anyway for their two days together, as this will surely help both of them greatly. Amelia thanked them for their support and care for her. Amelia stated that she really doesn't know when she gets like that, once the overpowering feeling of darkness overshadows her, she sees nothing else. Aunty Jackie encouraged her to keep her focus only on the beautiful baby she is about to bring into the world.

Two days later Amelia took a train from London back to Little Sister Care home convent in Dundee Scotland where she lived with the Little Sister of the Poor Nuns. Two weeks later, Aunty Jackie stated that she got another call from Reverend Sister Maria that Amelia gave birth to a beautiful baby girl named *Amoris*. Sister Maria requested that she come down to the convent with her husband immediately.

Aunty Jackie explained to Sister Marie that she was not in excellent condition to travel down to Scotland, for she was almost due with the twins and on bed rest. Sister Maria then said that she needs someone that can decide regarding Amelia and her baby, and she told her that her husband, Ben, is Amelia's uncle. He is in a better position to decide on anything concerning Amelia. Aunty Jackie stated that she asked her if Amelia and the baby are fine, and Sister Maria answered with a calm voice that her husband will see them and will report back to her.

Reverend Sister Maria continued to request from her to have her husband Ben hurries down to the convent immediately. Aunty Jackie stated that she had mixed feelings about Sister Maria's tone and message but dismissed them and stayed positive. She hurried her husband Ben out on his way to Scotland to visit Amelia and the new baby.

Aunty Jackie continued to narrate all that her husband told her happened from the time he got to the convent. She said that he told her he got to Little Sister's convent late evening. After registering himself at the primary entrance, he observed that one nun at the entrance made a phone call. Moments later, he observed four nuns walk by him with gloomy faces, and the fifth came out and walked towards him with a new baby in her hand. His heart was cut but he told himself that he is a man and must comfort himself.

The nun with the baby in her hand introduced herself as Reverend Sister Maria. She handed the baby to him and stated to him, this is Amoris, the baby delivered by Amelia. Aunty Jackie said that Ben told her that all he heard was Sister Maria told him with a calm voice that she is so sorry to tell him that Amelia, his niece gave up her ghost two hours after delivering the baby. Sister Maria continued to explain to him that at one point Amelia was ecstatic with her new baby and told them that the baby's name is Amoris, but the next thing they experienced were complications and Amelia was fighting for her life; that they did everything they could and still they lost her.

Aunty Jackie stated that Ben told her he looked at the baby and looked at Sister Maria, looked at the baby again, and looked at Sister Maria, with tears streaming down his masculine face. All he heard himself yell out was No, No, No! What will he tell Amelia's mother in Nigeria? What will he tell his pregnant wife Jackie? What will he do with this baby, especially now with him having no stable job? God, why! Why! Why! If this is a dream; could he beg God or someone and anyone around to knock him out of it? That the baby in his hands was almost dropped when Sister Maria gently touched him on the shoulder – it brought him back to his senses.

Sister Maria requested that he come with her to her office to fill out some paperwork that she needs about every contact and next of Kin to Amelia. Aunty Jackie stated that Ben was still holding Baby Amoris in his hand when he quietly followed Reverend Sister Maria to her office. That it was in that office while filling out the forms with a shaky hand and voice that Ben informed Sister Maria of the ironic story surrounding Amelia. He told her that the only contact Amelia has in Nigeria is her mother, Mrs. Dorcas Nwafor, popularly known as Mama Enugwu, and that Amelia's mom is his sister.

He gave the full address of Amelia's mom and continued to narrate to Sister Maria that Amelia was in a domestic violent marriage back in Nigeria, for she was being battered by her husband Joe in Nigeria. When the opportunity to study nursing here in Scotland came through, the family saw it as a breakthrough and an answer to their prayer. They wanted to send Amelia far away from her husband for all the back-and-forth safety measures that were not working. After each beating episode Amelia usually runs home to her family and her family will beat Joe and her husband up, and they will keep Amelia home with them until her husband will come and plead for her back. According to custom, Amelia will go back home with him. Each time this happens Amelia will return to her husband against her family's advice.

Desperately, her family concluded that to smuggle her out of Nigeria far away from her abusive husband will be the only answer. Amelia got married at a very young age to an equally immature man and had two children, a girl and a boy, by her husband who claimed he was exhibiting youth exuberance behaviors. Joe, Amelia's husband, was drowning all his frustrations behind alcohol and drunkenness and when saturated with alcohol usually comes home and batters Amelia beyond recognition. Usually, when the beating occurs and Amelia runs home, she will stay home with her family until her husband sobers up. Once sober he will come to Amelia's family and his family members with wine to beg for his wife back and they will send Amelia back with him.

Ben continued to tell Sister Maria that it never takes long after Amelia returns to her husband that another worst beating will happen. Subsequently, Amelia was hiding away all emotional abuse and bruises that Joe inflicts on her from her family. They found her to be protecting the man that blatantly robbed her of her human dignity; her self-esteem shattered by a drunken self-centered husband, which explains why she conceals his excesses from everyone.

The last straw was when Amelia's only sister who does not take any nonsense from any man observed Amelia with a battered face. She asked Amelia what happened and Amelia refused to say what happened to her. Amelia's sister told the family that she sneaked into Amelia and Joe's home unexpectedly and gave Joe the worst beating of his life, and she dared him to tell his fellow Nigerian men, who gave him that beating.

Culture-wise, Joe will never tell other people that a woman entered his home and gave him such a beating that left visible marks on him for that stripped him of his manhood if he had any left. Aunty Jackie said that Ben told Sister Maria that it was at this point that Amelia's family gave her a mandate not to go back to her husband for fear that it will be her corpse that will come back to them next. The family feared that after the humiliating beating episode of Joe he might try to exact revenge on Amelia. Another roadblock for Amelia was that in Nigerian culture children belong to the man; Amelia could not leave with her children. The only best option was that she will go with the families' mandate to fly abroad and study and must leave her two children behind for the man. Amelia was at a crossroads. Should she save her life or abandon her two children to the man? Amelia did not agree with the family's decision to leave her husband.

While this turmoil was going on, she got a scholarship to travel to England to study nursing abroad. With this news, her family convinced her to take a break from the man. They convinced her that the scholarship was an excellent way to conceal her from him for a while. So Amelia agreed with the family's decision to keep her whereabouts confidential so that her husband will not locate her. Aunty Jackie said that Ben told Sister Maria to whom he was narrating Amelia's plight to see why he himself said this irony is beyond him – that Amelia's family sent her to this convent residential home without the husband's knowledge or consent.

The husband, after the sobering period, went to Amelia's family to beg for his wife back as usual; when he got there they gave him his two children and told him that he no longer has the privilege to take back Amelia as a wife. He was also told to make sure he understands that it was serious that Amelia is not with them either. He accused them of kidnapping his wife, of shattering and breaking his family apart.

They told him to go back with his two beautiful children and better take excellent care of them or else. Aunty Jackie said that Ben told her he narrated Amelia's story with tears flowing down his face as Reverend Sister Maria patiently listened. He told her that this was the root of the emotional instability that Amelia was displaying while with them. For Amelia discovered she was pregnant with another child when she got to England; she believed that what was to be for her good turned into chaos. She found herself in a hopeless, senseless crossroad. Amelia began agonizing on her mistakes, guilt, the feeling of being lied to, being alienated in a strange land, with complications surrounding her studies and a new baby, and deep concerns surrounding the two children left behind.

Amelia kept everything to herself, refused to eat, and cried non-stop to the point of your calling for us to pick her up. From the first day Amelia entered England she was sick, kept everything to herself, loved to stay in the dark, cried always, and always asked Jackie, my wife, when does it end. She also had pregnancy complications which did not help matters; again while she was not only dealing with being pregnant she dropped out of the nursing program until after her baby was born. Stopping school was so traumatic for her as she cried for facing disappointments, misjudged intentions, deep-rooted pain and hurt that she always asked my wife Jackie: When will the pain ease away?

Aunty Jackie said that Ben asked Sister Maria how he told his pregnant wife about Amelia. What will he tell Amelia's mother in Nigeria that smuggled her out of the country to elude an abusive husband? Amelia was running away from death and her race brought her to death. Sister Maria asked Ben to look at that beautiful baby in his hand and know that God's plan differs from man's plan. Sister Maria was consoling Ben, he felt light-headed, and suddenly darkness enveloped him; he only felt the baby being taken from him then everything faded away.

The next thing was that Uncle Ben woke up with his wife Aunty Jackie staring down at him as he lay still in the hospital bed. "What happened? Why am I here?" he asked. Aunty Jackie said that she was quiet for a while with tears streaming down her face; then she told him that he had been in a coma for the past seven days. She told him she cannot even explain to him how she got there. She thanked God that he came back, for she really cannot handle their twins alone. Aunty Jackie said that Ben said to her: "You know what happened to Amelia then?" She answered, "Yes, Sister Maria told me that Amelia had baby Amoris safe and sound but hours later when they went to check on Amelia they discovered she was cold and lifeless." "What about baby Amoris?" Ben asked? Sister Maria said that Amoris remains at the convent with them for her to take care of him.

Ben asked what they planned in place for the burial arrangement of Amelia. Aunty Jackie stated that she gave them permission to do whatever they see fit. By 7:00 am of the second day Sister Maria contacted her at the hospital where they transported Ben to say that they had permission from their Superior to cremate Amelia and that was what they did. I thanked them and by 9 pm that same day they moved unannounced to a London hospital that will accept an undocumented patient.

Aunty Jackie said that she moved him yet again to the current hospital where they were more familiar with, and because of the movements she lost contact with Sister Maria because she literally had been staying at the hospital with Uncle Ben the whole time. They shut her phone off, and the worst was that she had no money at all to settle any bill as they speak right there.

Aunty Jackie stated that Uncle Ben encouraged her that all will be well for not long after that they discharged Ben from the hospital. They moved in with a friend temporarily, for they lost the apartment they lived in before all that started. Early one morning Aunty Jackie said that she woke Uncle Ben up asking him, "Are we going to live here as squatters when our twins arrive?" She continued to ask Ben to look at their life for they are homeless and Ben was with no stable job, Aunty Jackie said that she suggested to Ben that they should go back to Nigeria. Aunty Jackie said that Uncle Ben exploded with anger, telling her to stay focused; that he never wanted to hear the mention of going back to Nigeria from her mouth ever again.

Aunty Jackie said that she told him, "Whatever you say, Ben. You will not hear me comment on that again." Two days passed by and Aunty Jackie said that she went into labor and Ben rushed her to the hospital where their twin boys were born. About eighteen months after the birth of the twins, the nuns were able to locate Jackie and Ben. Sister Maria informed them that they had sent baby Amoris to her grandmother, Mrs. Dorcas Okafor in Nigeria. They explained that they could not locate Jackie and Ben for a long time.

IN HER OWN VOICE

Aunt Jackie later found out that Sister Maria and the nuns tried to locate them but could not; their only option was to send baby Amoris to Amelia's mother, Mrs. Dorcas Okafor, in Nigeria. Back in Nigeria, I vividly recall always wearing a red jumpsuit that I loved so much where red became my favorite color. The nuns dressed me in a beautiful red jumpsuit, put a tag on me, and mailed me like a letter to my grandmother in Nigeria.

Ironically, little did the nuns know the exchange of life they were the conduit of in accomplishing for my mother's family who smuggled their daughter Amelia off to England in search of safety and freedom but over there, Amelia met her death. In return, her family received a brand fresh life packaged in a new baby, Amoris. My mother's family lost their daughter but God mysteriously gave them a fresh life which none of the family members saw as a miracle of God because of them being drowned in the pain of their loss.

Chapter Two

Meaning of the Name Amoris

Mrs. Dorcas Okafor, my grandmother, popularly known as Mama Enugwu, was very much respected in the city of Enugwu. Culturally, any young man who married a new wife sent his wife to the oldest and virtuous mother in their family for a specified period to train the young on how to be a good wife and mother before she settled with her husband.

Uncle Valentine also known as Val, had brought his new young wife Comfort, or Commy to mama Enugwu for such training. Aunty Commy lived with mama Enugwu when I arrived at my grandmother's from abroad. Naturally, Aunty Commy became the mother to whom I clung. I became her primary duty while she trained to be a good wife and mother. I stuck on Aunty Commy like a stamp to an envelope. I would not allow anyone else near.

One Sunday afternoon, Uncle Val visited my grandmother, mama Enugwu. He had come to take his wife home to start their own family. When Aunty Commy explained why she was packing her belongings into a bag, I let out a screeching scream that startled all the adults present. I was screaming,

"Ngeso Commy Naa," (I will go home with Commy.)

Mama Enugwu tried every trick, plea, persuasion, even bribery, to shut me up, all to no avail. But when she got her koboko (a whiplash) I took to my heels still protesting,

"Ngeso Commy Naa." No matter how much my grandmother tried to stop me, I refused to yield. I rolled on the ground, held onto her left leg, until Uncle Val pleaded with Mama Enugwu, to let me go with them. He assured her that I would not be a problem at all. My grandmother permitted them to take me. I went and lived with Uncle Val and Aunty Commy.

Uncle Val was a farmer in the rural part of Nigeria, a place called Enugwu-Agidi. Uncle Val was the only son of his mother in a polygamous family. He had a sister named Mabel. Mabel, his sister, lived in Achala village of Enugwu-Agidi with her two young adult children Babe and Anayo. Mabel visited Uncle Val and Aunty Commy regularly, especially after I came to live with them. So, I got used to Aunty Mabel and her children. This gave Uncle Val a good opportunity to send me to go and live with his sister Mabel and her children.

While living with Aunty Mabel and her family in the village, her children engaged me in all the playground activities there were. One great playtime activity at that time was the moonlight game at the village square. All children gathered in a big round circle with lantern light in the middle. The older children told moonlight stories to the children who had gathered. The first moonlight story time in which I participated left an indelible mark in my mind.

Once I was introduced by Anayo as Amoris, their niece, one saucy girl, opined,

"Amoris? What on earth is that? A name or something else?" This saucy big-mouthed girl added for emphasis, "I have never heard anybody called by that name." Embarrassed, Anayo paused for a while, turned to me as if in search of the answer to that question. I gave him no answer. Rather, I shrugged my shoulders in disgust and wonderment and calmly walked away from Anayo and the circle, deeply hurt.

I moved back with Uncle Val after two years living with Aunty Mabel. At this time, the couple had had a daughter, and I became the baby's nanny. I babysat Nkem. My main job was to carry her while her parents went to the farm. I teamed up with other young people who babysat their little brothers and sisters. We always gathered in one compound with babies that we were watching. There we played together and kept an eye on the babies.

One day, I took Nkem to the gathering at a neighbor's compound and for a moment my eyes were turned, and I heard Nkem let out a screeching cry. I turned and I yelled at one boy standing next to Nkem when she cried,

"What did you do to my sister? To my astonishment, the boy said,

"Bia, Amoris, (Come, Amoris) or whatever you call yourself." He said my name with much disdain remarking that he did not know why any sensible parent would give a child such a meaningless name. That young man's statement paralyzed me. I opened my mouth to say something, but nothing came out. I quietly went to Nkem, picked her up, and went back to my Uncle Val's home. I said nothing about that incident to my Uncle Val.

But from then on, I recoiled into myself. I said little when I was around other children for fear that someone might pick on me, get offended and throw some embarrassing questions at me. I became very observant and I determined to locate anyone who had a similar name as I did. But I found none around. In this culture, names were meaningfully chosen and given to children. And every child knew the meaning of his or her name. This time I asked myself the question,

"Okay, I am called Amoris; what does Amoris mean anyway?" I got no answer. No one around knew the meaning of my name, that hurt deeply.

Soon, I found myself living with another uncle in the city. Uncle Ejike, his wife and four children lived at Udi Road, Enugu. I never knew how it happened or who sent me to his home. It was here that I started my primary school career.

The first year I lived with Uncle Ejike was the hardest. It was the beginning of a new school year, in September 1970, the year the Nigerian civil war ended. Uncle Ejike had bought school uniforms and original metal school boxes for his four children. He bought none for me. My uncle's house at Udi Road was behind the primary school building. I went to school in whatever clothes I had then. No one was responsible for either my school uniform or the metal school box for my books. Elementary schooling was free at that time under the nationwide Universal Free Primary Education (UPE) program.

The school provided me with notebooks and workbooks, so I carried my books in a brown paper bag. I continued to attend school in non-approved school dressing. Every day, my teacher humiliated me in front of the class where she spanked me for not wearing the school uniform. The metal school boxes fascinated me a lot and I longed for one. After one month I still did not get any school uniform and I was given a cutoff date after which I would no longer be allowed into school without school uniform. Each time I got spanked at school I would go to my uncle and ask him if he could please provide me with a school uniform and metal box. I pleaded for the uniform because without it, I got spanked at school daily. He responded that he did not have money to buy them for me and that I should wait. It appeared that his wait time was never ending.

Behind our street, Udi Road, there was a garbage dump. Children usually went there to scavenge for finders' keepers' items. Sometimes one found usable things thrown away. Early one Saturday morning, I went to throw away some garbage and saw a rusted metal school box in that dump. I took it and ran home happily. It had a small hole at the base and the rain that had fallen a few days before and soaked it, had caused it to rust even more. I painted the inside to mask the rust and the bad smell it exuded then I layered the inside with thick paper to cover the hole at the bottom. Now, I had a metal school box.

A few days later, my grandmother, Mama Enugwu, whom I respectfully addressed as Mama Nnukwu, (Big Mama) came visiting from the village. I was incredibly happy and told her about my need for a school uniform. She gave me the money for it. That was how I got a school uniform.

My joy that my grandmother had come and could supply my needs was short-lived because she went back to the village a couple of days later and I continued to live with my uncle. Meanwhile, my classmates often asked me the meaning of my name: a question I always dreaded since I did not know what my name meant. I think that in many cultures, there is something about the name given to a child. The name parents give to their children speaks into the children's future. I was the only child around who bore the name, Amoris. In my part of Nigeria, every parent gave their children native names that meant something good. Most of the time, names were assigned to a child based on how God had been faithful or blessed the family. Take for instance, names like Chidinma or Chiamaka, (God is good). When a Christian name is chosen, such names come from the bible or book of names of saints. We have examples such as Emmanuel, Joshua, and many more. My mother named me Amoris, and she was not there to explain the meaning to anyone.

When I went into high school, my French teacher solved the puzzle. She explained to the entire class that my name was a Latin word that meant Love. She further taught us that both Latin and French meaning of Amoris was Love. I took a very deep breath and sighed,

"Wow!"

"You mean Amoris means Love?" I wanted my teacher to confirm.

"Yes!" she said.

What a relief! Now, I can answer this question anytime, anywhere. One major hurdle in my life had been removed. But more questions surfaced.

"Where is your mother?" "With whom do you live?" I do not remember answering any of these questions. All I know was that I always dreamt of having a mother or father like other children. I then told myself that if wishes were horses, my preferences would never end anyway.

Chapter 3

Early Life in Nigeria

In Nigeria, I was moved around from homes of one maternal uncle or aunty to another. I intuitively realized that it was only my grandmother, Mama Nnukwu, who truly and sincerely stepped up to provide my needs as a responsibility. In most of the family homes I lived in, I went there out of necessity. At first, I felt much anxiety because I knew that soon my deficiency would be exposed. I hated to stick out like a sore thumb.

In my childhood days in Nigeria, Christmas was children's favorite holiday season. Most parents tailored new Christmas clothes for their children at this time. But for me, Christmas time was my nightmare in those early years. The severity of the nightmare depended on the family with whom I lived at the time. One Christmas time while I was living with my uncle Ejike and his family at Enugu, we spent Christmas in the city. Why we even spent Christmas that year in the city was beyond my comprehension. Many families usually traveled to the village to spend the Christmas holidays. My family did the same. During Christmas holidays, families rejoined, and cousins would meet and know each other. My grandmother always provided a new Christmas outfit for me whenever I returned to the village. This Christmas turned out to be the worst Christmas of my young life. Two days to Christmas it became real to me that I would not get any new outfit.

Of course, Uncle Ejike made new outfits for his children but none for me. I did not waste my breath, asking him why. I felt so abandoned and helpless that while other children in the compound were jubilating and getting ready to show off their newly tailored Christmas outfit for church on Christmas day, I sought a hiding place. I distanced myself from other children and recoiled into my shell. Whenever I was not doing house chores, I went to my hiding place and sobbed. I resorted to praying for a miracle to happen such that my grandmother would show up in the city. That Christmas, my prayer was not answered. That Christmas season stood out as a sore memorial etched in my soul. I advised myself to accept the truth that I was an orphan and belonged to nobody. Lonely and sad, I cried a lot just as I used to see my grandmother cry. I wished that I would settle somewhere or belong somewhere. I knew I was an inconvenience to relatives who kept me in their homes.

I recall one experience when I was living with Uncle Val and Aunty Commy. I was about five or six years old when the Nigerian civil war broke out in 1967. Neither Uncle Val nor Aunty Commy was home when our town was evacuated. I saw people carrying bundles of their property on their heads. Everybody was running through the small pathway trying to escape from the airplane above that was bombing and killing people randomly. I just got up and followed the families that were running away from the horror of the war. I just followed the crowd and slept whenever night fell. The families usually gathered in an open school building for the night. I always attached myself to one of the families. The refugees ran from the bombing airplanes flying overhead for about two weeks or more. When we came to a lake or a significantly deep stream, each family began to take their children across the water. That was when reality set in that I belonged to no one. I went into the water with no one to hold my hand and I attempted to cross that stream. I was young and ignorant of the danger that lurked in the water which was too deep for me. To cap it all, I could not swim either.

Even the water rejected me and refused to take me. After the water threw me up into the air once, twice and three times, out of nowhere someone fished me out. I was laid flat on the ground and pressed so that water gushed out of my mouth and lungs and I gasped for breath. I did not drown. I stayed with the group until Uncle Val's family found me and took me. I remained with Uncle Val's family through the three-year civil war before I saw my grandmother again.

During the same war, I saw an airplane bomb the marketplace one sunny afternoon that Aunty Commy had taken me to the market. On my right was a pregnant woman who had been cut horizontally into two with one half of her going one way still gyrating up and down. Her stomach had been cut open with the baby inside going through the same fate. The baby's tiny body was twisting up and down before it finally stopped. The sight caused me to pass out. I did not know how I got into the bunker, where we always hid when the fighter planes and bombers attacked the civilians.

During that war, I suffered severe malnutrition. My stomach was swollen. That condition put me on the priority list of beneficiaries from the missionaries' relief program of cornmeal and other relief food sent to the refugees. In all this, I looked forward to seeing my grandmother again. The only thing that smoothened the wilderness of pain and trauma of that war was that my grandmother found Uncle Val's family towards the end of the war, and she took me with her back to our village.

Chapter 4

Life with Grandma

My life with grandma can be illustrated with a favorite nugget that Evangelist Joy Osueke Rolle shared on the tribe prayer line recently. It was the lesson of that nugget amply applied by Mama Nnukwu that kept me focused when I wanted to quit. That nugget stated that the future belonged to those who saw the possibilities before they unfolded. While fear was a dead end, faith always had a future. When one turned on faith; light illuminated the situation and fear ran away. To the reader of *Broken, But not Beaten*, I say, Turn on your view right now!

I was named Amoris by my mother; the name means Love. I reminded myself that if my mother went through unimaginable obstacles at the time of my birth as my family narrated to me but she could see me as a loving, lovable child and gave me the name, Amoris, then who am I not to hold on to life and all its battles? This line of reasoning transformed me into a curious but highly conservative young woman. I questioned everything happening around me. I questioned my confused life, sorrow, agony, blessings, and emotional catastrophe. Still, in all that, I had gratefulness because I was living with Mama Nnukwu, who had received me back and held me close as if her entire life depended on having me. I was about nine years when I noticed my grandmother's agonizing tears flowing down her cheeks when people asked her questions, especially when such questions centered on whose child I was. The person who asked the question would then quietly answer their own question with

"Oh, this is Amelia's child? "Ewuo nwam oooo," meaning "Ouch! My child oooo! And the woman would cross her two hands on her chest in a sorrowful, sympathetic gesture. When I looked at my grandmother, more tears flowed down, and I would feel worse than death if I knew how death felt. I usually waited for the women to leave, and then I would bombard Mama Nnukwu with questions like,

"Why are you crying?" "Why are those women beating their chests, feeling sorry for us?" "Who is my father?" "Where is my mother?" The more questions I asked her, the more she cried. She never answered my questions; she only sat uptight and gazed ahead to wherever I sat with her tears rolling down non-stop. She got my attention in this way, for I loved my grandmother very much. Once I saw her crying like that. I got up, sat next to her, and wiped her eyes with my hand. I would beg her to stop weeping. Then, I would promise her that I would stop asking her questions that made her cry. That always worked and she stopped the tears. On my part, I tried not to ask any more questions.

The result was that consequently, I developed the attitude of not talking much of the time. I rather became a sponge who soaked up the happenings around me, I decoded these events to suit my life challenges at different times. I became extremely observant so much so that as young as I was, I devised a way to make sure that my grandmother never encountered situations that reminded her of anything that would make her cry.

Whenever someone visited her and I figured that this person would pose the question, I disappeared and came back only after that person had left. In the absence of details of my birth and background, I began to create illusions in my head; maybe I killed my mother at my birth. Maybe Mama Nnukwu cried often because my mother was still overseas but refused to come back home. But why on earth couldn't I have a mother like other children? I asked myself. Where was my father, by the way? Every child has a father, why couldn't anyone breathe the word 'father' to me? Why was it a taboo to ask about my father? I became an introvert by choice as a defense mechanism. I chose not to open to people. That was my beautiful way of navigating through this wicked world.

After the war, I lived with grandma for a while before she sent me back to Enugu to live with Uncle Ejike again. I protested that I wanted to stay in the village with her, but she argued convincingly that I had to go back to school. My grandma confessed that schools in the city would better prepare me for the future. I moved around several more times before my high school career ended. I got accepted to one of the best boarding high schools for girls in Enugu.

In the boarding schools, we had monthly visiting days. I never got anyone to visit me on such days. This situation brought back dark memories of loneliness and rejection which I thought I had successfully repressed. During visiting hours on such days, I stayed in the dorm. I did not want to watch other children with their families. In the middle of the night on such days, my pillow often became my sobbing companion, and tears became my tasty drink. I was always able to soak my pillow with tears before the crack of dawn. I cried because it seemed that no one loved me. Why do I not have a mother to call my own; Why do I not have a father of my own? Why was life so unfair to me? Why is no one telling me who I am and why I am on the face of this earth? Visiting days at our boarding high school became the most traumatic day for me. Sometimes I saw a flash of the woman killed by a bomb during the war. It usually came like a vision and then it would fade away. I usually saw these flashes when I was down, depressed, and miserable. On such visiting days, I would hide anywhere that was big enough to conceal me to avoid getting those flashbacks.

When I got tired of playing hide and seek, I started visiting aunts and uncles that lived in the same city. I begged them to come and visit me on visiting days so that I would at least have someone there for me. My effort seemed to work somehow because on the next school visiting day, a woman and her daughter came to visit me. They said they were from my father's family. I was shocked, especially when I remembered how Mama Nnukwu used to cry her eyes out anytime I inquired about my father. I had been craving all along to have someone to visit me on visiting days, and here I was with visitors to see me, but no, not from my father's family. How on earth did they know that I was in that school? Did they know me? How would they identify me when they saw me? If these people knew where to find me, then my father must know where to locate me. I received them respectfully as I was raised up to do but I did not volunteer any information nor ask any questions. Intuitively I knew that my grandmother would not approve of their visit; therefore, I thrashed everything that they had brought me. I said to myself, maybe our father knew where I was and had been spying on me without anyone knowing. I recounted the event to my grandma but as I narrated the story, her mood changed. The next thing that I observed was tears flowing down her face. I immediately told her that I did not tell them anything and did not eat the food they gave me. With that information, my grandmother gradually stopped crying and became happy again as she used to whenever I was with her.

My visiting day desire to be visited by someone continued. I devised a different approach to the visiting day drama. I got together with a group of sympathetic young friends and classmates. We organize ourselves, six friends in all. Three of us never got visitors, while the other three had families who visited them regularly, bringing an abundance of food and supplies. We shared the food and all the things that their families brought them equally. That group became my family until I left boarding school at 18 years old. Again, I felt that life mistreated me. To me, the world was a cruel, hopeless, tasteless, and merciless place. I complained this to God any time I got the chance. Now, as I retrospectively reflect on these events from a mature perspective, I dare to say that many a time God turns to our good, the very evil with which the enemy intended to harm us. I believe these trials of my young life have become the blueprint training to nurture my adult life. As I came into adulthood, I then devised a positive way to shield me from any pain that I want to avoid. More importantly, as an adult, in all situations, I believe that God is in control.

Chapter 5

Knowledge of having Siblings

I kept much to myself a lot to avoid painful flashbacks of past experiences once I was less occupied with meaningful activity. Consequently, studying my book round the clock became my favorite hobby. If I were not reading my books, I would have this fleeting momentary sadness that would overwhelm my entire body. At such moments I re-lived the time that I almost drowned but did not. I would wonder why I did not drown in that water, "Did God just keep me alive to continue living this life of loneliness, rejection, and disappointments? I drifted back and forth but I often reflected on the bible stories that I had learned in church. The case of Joseph who was thrown into the pit by his brothers and was later sold as a slave to foreigners resonated a lot with me. Joseph went to jail for a crime he did not commit. But by providence he interpreted Pharaoh's dream and consequently, he got promoted to the second highest position in Egypt straight from prison. Even as I mused on these connections, I would see the image of the pregnant woman that got split into two that I had witnessed during the civil war. In this tragedy, I saw how a mother hung her life on a thread just to bring a new life into the world. I would see the bloody environment when a child is born in the delivery room. Then, yet soon after the new baby emerged from the bloody and messy process and was cleaned up and handed to the mother, the mother would forget all the pains and bloody sacrifice. She is filled with joy.

It appeared I loved to drown myself in the events of my life alternating between sad and happy ones depending on what I remembered at the time. My mind would wander back to the last time I visited Uncle Ejike in the city. I had gone there to invite him to try and visit me in the boarding school for the school visiting day was fast approaching. When I got to the compound, I met Julie, my relative with whom I had developed an emotional attachment when I lived with Uncle Ejike earlier. Julie was happy to see me and ran to me and asked after my boarding school experience. Then she told me that Mama Nnukwu's granddaughter Chinenye was visiting at the same time and was inside with uncle Ejike's family. Julie then whispered to me that she heard her parents say that Chinenye was my blood sister. I asked Julie to get out of my way. I was wondering how I could have spent hours asking my grandmother questions about my siblings, and for answers, she gave me tears and nothing else. I agreed with Julie that I would act like I did not know anything, but that I should ask Chinenye to find out what she knew.

Later, as Julie and I were sitting on the steps of our house, Chinenye joined us. She requested me to run an errand to the store for her. She gave me some money to buy snacks for her and get candy for myself. I went and came back as fast as I could, so happy was I to meet someone that was said to be my sister. When I got back, I gave her the snacks, and I asked her excitedly,

"Is it true that you are my sister?" Chinenye, who was 13 years at the time, looked at me and then said,

"Yes, I am your sister." She then invited me to sit next to her, and she informed me that we had a brother, Chidi, who was older than I but younger than she was. She added that both of them lived with our father who had remarried. She narrated that their lives revolved around an evil stepmother. Sister Chinenye looked straight at me and assured me that I fared better living with Mama Nnukwu. I had mixed feelings about that statement. But I whispered,

"At least you have someone you call your brother with whom you are going through whatever is happening." I told her that I could not get information about anyone from Mama Nnukwu. In my head, I challenged the statement Chinenye made that I fared better where I was. I convinced myself that what everyone deemed a necessity is obviously different. I definitely did not know what my brother and Chinenye was experiencing at the hand of a stepmother, I shuddered at the thought that it must be horrific. Obviously one man's meat is another's poison.

We then exchanged information on how to reach one another. It was through that connection that she contacted me when our father died six years later. I sought permission from Mama Nnukwu to go to his funeral but did not get that. I consoled myself with the Word of God which says that before I was born, God had already called me by name and had already destined my life's purpose. Whatever someone goes through in life is only a training and guidance to enable one scale through the rigors of breath. If I stretch my faith and exercise patience, I will emerge victorious. I assured myself that the hardships of my life might break me but cannot kill me.

Chapter 6

Death of my Grandmother

I spent most of my time with my grandmother during my early years. I went everywhere with her and I watched her very closely learning all she did and valued. She prayed a lot and fasted often. She trained me in the habit of praying and fasting. Our lives at that time looked like we lived in the church. My grandmother, who was a woman leader in her protestant church denomination, took me to her church services. In this tradition, both young and old studied the bible and the miracles of God through prayers. Children were assigned bible passages to study and memorize. They were then required to publicly read out their bible verses, recite their bible verses before the congregation at various church events. People were often thrilled to see and hear the children read and recite the bible verses.

For one of these children's bible reading presentations, my grandmother instructed me to study and present a bible passage. I studied the Eight Beatitudes of the Sermon on the Mount found in Matthew 5:1-12. As I practiced these bible verses and read them out loud, the words embedded in my subconscious mind of how God blessed the humble, the meek, the poor. I learned how God ensured that the merciful received mercy and the peacemaker were called sons of God. He also comforted those who mourned. I was about 9 or 10 years old when these eternal words were planted deeply in me. They became principles that guided my decisions and framed the type of life I chose for myself. As I grew older and encountered trials that tended to break my heart, I applied these bible passages. I believed every word that I read in the bible. I consciously began to imitate humility.

If there was an argument between me and someone else, I would let go. I found myself practicing meekness and humility. Gradually, I found myself forgiving everything and everyone who offended me. I was no longer imitating these virtues. They had become part of my character. I believed that God was comforting me for not having any mother or father to call my own. My grandmother taught me to pray and fast for whatever I wanted out of life. Her deep-rooted lessons taken from the scriptures that she guided me to memorize and read in front of the church as a child formed the foundation of my entire existence.

My faith in God was tested not long after. Immediately I completed high school, my grandmother got extremely sick and was admitted to the hospital. I left my A-level program and went to stay with her. I stayed by her bedside for over a month. While I was with her at the hospital, she was concerned about me and what would become of me when she was gone.

Meanwhile, I just wanted her to get better. Hot tears gushed down her cheeks whenever she looked at me sitting by her bedside. She would not eat neither would I eat for we had no appetite. Those dreaded questions began all over again. What would become of Amoris? While I complained that she ate nothing, she complained to the doctors that her granddaughter had refused to eat and requested them to do something. I got caught in a drama of shedding sorrowful tears for my grandmother only that I never allowed her to see me cry. Then, I started praying fervently for her to get better. I reminded God that she was all I had.

One day my aunt Amara came to the hospital to visit my grandmother, her own mother. It occurred to me then, that my grandmother might not leave the hospital alive. She welcomed my aunty while I sat beside my grandmother. In my presence, she made my aunty promise her that she would inherit me and take care of me no matter what. My aunt promised her that she would take me and be responsible for me all the way. When I learned that my grandmother died, I was beside myself. I refused to be consoled and wanted to die. I became a walking dead, having lost the will to live. I went into shock for a period. I did not speak; I did not cry out loud. I simply maintained the same posture that I had seen my grandmother take for years with hot tears raining down my eyes. All I saw then was her face crying for help. Oh, she too has left me. So, this was why she sent me out briefly. She knew that her death was near. Why did she not let me say good-bye? Why did she never tell me who I was? Why was she always crying when I asked her questions about myself? Now that she was gone, who would answer my questions? I prayed that I may die with her, for I did not like the way my life was going. At her burial, I was still mute and was the child who gazed into the horizon; the child who saw only her grandma's weeping face. I refused to be consoled. I tried to jump into the grave with my grandmother, but friends and sympathizers succeeded in restraining me; they kept me restrained till the burial was completed. Why must anyone who came close to loving me die? I quickly answered my question by reminding me that I might have been broken, but God remembered me still.

Chapter 7

Inherited by Aunt Amara

I was about nine or ten years old when my grandmother requested Aunt Amara, my mother's only sister, to take me to the city to live with her. Aunt Amara had just returned from overseas after many years of studies. Aunt Amara took my cousin, Ijeoma, her brother's daughter and me, to live with her in Lagos, a large city in the western part of Nigeria. Having acquired higher education herself, my aunt's focus in life was on education. She believed that women deserved a chance to receive formal education just like men. She had promised my grandmother that she would ensure that both of us girls in her care would do well. My grandmother was relieved now that Amoris had somewhat a stable home. I was still my grandmother's responsibility. The difference was that I no longer had to go from one uncle's house to another. All decisions concerning me were made by my grandmother until that fateful day on her sickbed at the hospital when she formally handed me over to my aunt. That was the time that my aunt, in my presence, promised that she would inherit me. That was the moment my first stable home became official. My aunty was not married at that time and so had no children of her own.

Living with my aunt in the city, brought me a refreshing hope. She was a straightforward no-nonsense disciplinarian. She made her desires clear from the beginning. She demanded our diligence with our education. If we heeded her words and excelled in school, she would support us to any level of education we wanted. Well, I did not wait for her to repeat herself. I took the offer and ran before she changed her mind. I was an orphan and I had just won a jackpot. At school, I maintained the first place in my classes. My aunt scrutinized every report card I brought home to her. She checked every detail and noted my progress. If I ever lost the first position in any school subject, a rare occurrence, she would chastise me. I would then study harder and perform better. I continued to excel in school. My cousin, on the other hand, did not take the matter seriously.

To prove her position on academics, my aunt Amara sent a stern message to Ijeoma's parents, informing them that she would send Ijeoma back to them if she failed to apply diligence to her academics. My aunt warned that she would not accommodate someone who was not serious about her academic work. My aunt's action opened my eyes wider to the need to continue to stay on top of my academic studies. As an orphan, I had no place to be dropped off if I missed this rare opportunity. In my case, slacking or failing was not even a remote option. Later in my adult life, I heard a nugget on my prayer line by Evangelist Joy Osueke Rolle that failure was not constant and that whenever one failed in one thing today, one could succeed in the same thing the next day. Hence, I did not give failure a tiny chance in my education at all. I was already living an isolated lifestyle. I eliminated everything that interrupted my studies. I was grateful to God for a stable home, though sometimes, I regarded it as a home that was on shaky grounds because its stability hinged upon my success at school. My aunt did not tolerate any excuse for failure. At that point in time, her stubborn position on the matter did not make much sense to me. Today, I thank God for her drive and insistence on the value of education. Once I had a stable home under her roof, I was grateful. But I wanted more than just a stable home. I still did not have anything I called mine. It was always my grandmother's, my aunt's, or uncle's, and nothing else. I still felt that I was not anywhere yet.

For this reason, I was never comfortable with anyone visiting me at my aunt's residence. While in elementary school, I was always top in my class and my classmates flocked around me. They either needed my help with their schoolwork or just wanted to be my friend. There was one Martha; she was the same age as I was. Martha would not take no for an answer. One day, she requested to go home with me after school, and I turned down her request. Rather than turn back, she walked behind me, insisting I let her visit my home. Martha begged that she wanted to be my friend. My reply was that I did not want any friend. How could I explain to another child that I did not live with my parents but with my aunt? It was an abnormal arrangement in my understanding. Martha followed me until I chased her with a rock; only then did she turn and run home. But Martha would be back on the same drama the next day. All I knew was that I belonged to my aunt, Amara, who promised my grandmother that she would be responsible for me. I was not going to allow anything to disrupt that security arrangement that I enjoyed.

Chapter 8

Lagos: My First stable home

Lagos is made up of Nigerians from many cultural backgrounds. Although Nigerians who spoke different languages live in Lagos, Yoruba language is the local language and non-Yoruba are obligated to quickly learn and speak the language if they want to avail themselves of the richness of Lagos as a seaport and the most populated city in Nigeria. People speak the Yoruba language, especially at Yaba, Oyinbo, and Balogun markets, and on the streets. Many people from all over Nigeria migrate to Lagos, the then capital city of Nigeria, in search of good jobs, good school opportunities, and business ventures.

Aunty Amara, my mother's sister, had landed a great job as lecturer with the top of the line university in Nigeria. Once she secured her apartment in Lagos, she requested that my grandmother send Ijeoma, one of her oldest brother's daughters and me to her so that she could assist with our education. Ijeoma, my cousin and I lived with aunty Amara towards the end of our primary school years. From there, I entered the boarding high school and only went back to aunty Amara during the long vacations. The city of Lagos presented different challenges to us, especially in navigating through our education there. These challenges were in the areas of language, culture and religion. I became aware of the Muslim religion for the first time in Lagos. Challenges faced us in bargaining the prices of items in the market, and the public transportation structure. My first culture shock was at the open market where we went to buy groceries. Then, we experienced another culture shock with the Lagos city public bus ride system.

One day, aunty Amara had dropped Ijeoma and me at the famous Yaba market to buy groceries for dinner. Our list included two pounds of beef for 2,000 Naira, fresh tomatoes for 500 Naira, a tin of tomato paste for 100 Naira, and fresh green vegetables for 200 Naira. She had given us the money for the purchase and transportation fare money and had shown us where to catch the campus bus back home before she hurried back to her lecture that day. Ijeoma and I got the two-pound beef and asked the butcher how much it would cost. To our surprise, he demanded that we pay 5,000 Naira. Ijeoma looked at me, and I checked our list for the budget for beef that size. Aunty Amara had indicated that it would cost not more than 2,000 Naira. I started to bargain from bottom up like we Igbo did in the eastern part of the country. So, I offered to pay 1,000 Naira for the beef. To my shock, the butcher snatched the meat from Ijeoma, who was holding it at the time. He rained abuses on me.

"Orie Odaa" "Olochi" in Yoruba, meaning "Your head is not correct" "You are a thief." Then he calmly asked us to pay 2,000 Naira. We paid his final price, took the meat, and we were careful to ask other sellers for the final price of their items so as not to get into any more trouble. Once their quoted price tallied with the money we had, we paid. Soon, we mastered the Lagos bargaining system. In this system, both seller and buyer bargained downwards from the quoted price until buyer and seller met somewhere below which the seller would not go. The Igbo buyer on the other hand, bargained from their lowest price and moved up while the seller moved down until both seller and buyer met somewhere agreeable to both.

After we purchased all that we needed, we went to where Aunty Amara had asked us to wait for the campus bus. Here, we witnessed another memorable spectacle. There were lots of people at this bus stop when we arrived. Soon, I observed that before any bus fully stopped, the conductor would beckon people to come and enter his bus, which meanwhile had not stopped or packed. The bus would still be in motion while the conductor screamed "campus, campus." While Ijeoma and I waited for the bus to come to a complete stop, which never happened, we saw passengers, old and young, male and female; enter the bus from any opening of the bus. Some crawled in through the trunk. Others scampered through the windows. A few fought their way through the one and only main door. Soon, the bus filled up and the driver who never stopped nor packed the bus for a minute, zoomed off. We watched in utter dismay, completely flabbergasted, as four campus buses got filled up in this manner and left for the campus, our destination. It was getting dark and it became a matter of doing like the Romans or walking home. We chose the former; we jumped into the next bus from the trunk. My cousin and I also had to master the local language because most of the school children conversed in Yoruba language or Pigeon English when they were outside the classrooms. Of course, formal English was the official medium of instruction but during recess, children communicated in the local language. We needed to learn the language as fast as we could to make progress in our academic and social life as students.

When we were set to get into high school, Aunty Amara specifically instructed us to work hard to get accepted into the schools of our choices. That done, she would pay all fees till we got the highest height we could academically reach. She warned that whoever failed would not continue to live with her. To me, failure was not an option. So, I took that warning seriously because I did not have anywhere to go, I called home. I studied extremely hard and got acceptance letters from all three high schools to which I had applied. Ijeoma, on the other hand, did not get accepted into any high school. Aunty Amara kept her promise and sponsored my high school education even though the boarding school I chose to attend was in the eastern part of the country, hundreds of miles from Lagos where I lived with her. This explained why I did not have visitors on my school's visiting days. My grandmother lived then in the village when I was in boarding high school. I spent short school breaks with her in the village. I spent long vacations in Lagos with Aunty Amara and her husband, for she got married at this time. I had just completed high school and wanted to get into an Engineering program in college. This desire did not materialize right away so I quickly started an A-level program before Mama Nnukwu fell sick. I abandoned everything and went to stay with her at the hospital. It was while I was staying with her in the hospital that Aunty Amara visited her. Right in my presence, Mama Nnukwu had made her daughter, Aunty Amara promise her that she would inherit me. I sat there and heard Aunty Amara promise her that she would take care of me. Mama Nnukwu made a second request of my aunty. She demanded that Aunty Amara send me back to my school program and not stay in the hospital anymore. She wanted Aunty Amara to find someone else to stay with her. Aunty Amara persuaded me to go back to Lagos for my exams. In retrospect, Mama Nnukwu knew she was approaching her end and she did not want me to witness that event.

I returned to Lagos and took my A-Level exams. My grandmother died the very day I completed my A-level exams. The loss of my grandmother got me a permanent home with Aunty Amara. I knew that once she had promised Mama Nnukwu, she would keep me.

With that assured, I entertained no more anxiety in that area. From then on, I confidently informed anyone who cared to know that I lived in Lagos with my aunty, Amara. After my grandmother's death, I spent all my vacations in Lagos which by this time had become my permanent home.

Chapter 9

Overcoming Emotional Meltdown Phase

About two years after my grandmothers' death, my life regressed into an emotional wreck. Then, I was never able to explain my strange mood swings. Later in life, I listened to a teaching on Self-Esteem by Apostle Patience Oti. It was after I heard that teaching that I understood what had happened to me years before. I share this aspect of my experience to help others decode themselves and break out of whatever they are experiencing. At that time, I went back to asking questions about my very existence. Who was I? I felt so much sorrow and cried a lot. I loved to isolate myself, not talk to anyone; I ate less because I had no appetite for food. I was able to hide my hurt by not crying out loud when I was in grief about anything. I started more passionately to seek answers to the question of who I was. If I met anyone who knew my mother, I would ask what they knew about my mother. I recall asking Aunty Amara about my mom. She just looked sternly at me but gave me no answer. I knew better not to ask again. I feared my aunty very much. She had to instruct me on something once and that was final.

One vacation period, Aunty Jackie's daughter, Adaku, who was also my cousin, arrived from the Eastern part of Nigeria to spend her vacation with us in Lagos. While staying with us, she informed me that her mother had intimated her that she, her mother, had been my mother's best friend and she knew a lot about my mother. I became close with Adaku and solicited her help in my predicament where neither my grandmother nor my Aunty Amara would share any information about my birth with me. We agreed that she would probe her mother for answers. This move paid off. Through Adaku I discovered that I was born in Scotland. Armed with this information, I wrote her mother Aunty Jackie for information about my birth and early beginnings. Aunty Jackie graciously provided me quite a lot about my mother. She even provided me with my birth certificate. Before then, I did not know my birth date. It delighted me much to learn from her that my mother was very charming and that I looked just like her. I added that I acted just like my mother. I had inherited her spirit of meekness. This explained why her husband battered her so much. On that note, I swore that I would never marry a man who would lay a finger on me. I determined that I would not be the battered wife my mother was.

Meanwhile, while I was searching for my true self, I continued to wallow in deep depression. I loved to stay in the dark. I kept to myself and loved it. I lost weight because

I ate little. I slept any time I was not studying. I was still able to function because I dared not slack in my schoolwork. I subsequently got accepted into the University of Lagos. True to her promise to my grandmother, my aunty funded my education all the way through the university. But I stayed in my depressed mode for over two years without even knowing how or what got me out of it. All I knew was that I had encountered my grandmother in a dream one night. In that encounter, I had insisted that I would follow her wherever she was going. Of course, she turned and started walking away from me. I insisted on following her, even when she instructed me to go back. When she got frustrated with my stubbornness, she took off one of her shoes, and threatened to hit me with it if I did not go back. Realizing that she was serious, I said, "Okay, I will go back." When I turned to run back, I opened my eyes. I was disappointed that this was a dream. Miraculously, from then on, I gradually began to come out of the red zone. I stopped feeling angry and sad much of the time. I believe and I testify that my coming out of the emotional pit into which I had fallen was a combination of the dream where my grandmother chased me from following her and the privilege I had to listen to the teachings on Self Esteem by Apostle Dr. Patience Oti, on the TRIBE prayer line. I did not only listen to her teachings, I practiced whatever the teaching of the Word of God instructed. In life, one's ability to overcome the disappointments of life depends a great deal on knowledge acquired and one's readiness and willingness to act on the instruction received.

Chapter 10

College life and Meeting Suitors

Many times, what we passionately seek eludes us when we seek that with a confused mind. I had so passionately pursued the resolution of all my life's difficulties that I drowned myself further in my studies. At the university studying Math, I pretended that my adverse circumstances were nonexistent. My college life revolved around waking up every morning and dashing off to the cafeteria for breakfast and then walking to the science center for morning lectures. I would then leave the lecture halls and head straight to the library. From the library I went to the cafeteria, and back to my dorm to sleep. The only change occurred on the weekend when I went to church on Sunday and back to bed at night. On weekends, I went home to spend time with my Aunty Amara, who was now married and had a beautiful daughter I was proud to call my baby sister.

One of the first things Aunty Amara did for me after she inherited me was to convert me to the Catholic faith. She had become a Catholic while studying abroad in Rome. With my grandmother, I had gone faithfully to a protestant church. Aunty Amara took me to the priest of the Catholic Church on campus to baptize me into the Catholic faith. Before I was baptized though, I had to take a new name. I requested the priest to satisfy my innermost desire to pick a native name instead of the name of a saint as I was supposed to. I was filled with joy when the priest obliged me. Aunty Amara wanted to know what name I wanted and why? I explained that I wanted the name Uzodinma, which means "the good way." I explained that while I was in elementary school, my school mates made fun of my name, Amoris. My classmates had made so much fun of my foreign name that I longed for a meaningful local name. I added that this new baptismal name should be my middle name. My aunty approved of my choice, and once baptized, I became a Catholic. From then on, during the weekends, I would go home and attend church services with my family and return to my campus dorm after services.

Things worked out for me in mysterious ways. I did not know that the very name that I thought was bad for me just because people exhibited their ignorance when they thought they were laughing at my name. The name, Amoris means Love. It was the meaning of my name that mysteriously paved the way for me in the spiritual realm. My name Amoris stands out, and in return, it makes me stand out. As I retraced my path in life, I realized that I was more favored and blessed than I had thought. A deep reflection on my life revealed to me that some things I thought were happening to me were not real.

What was happening physically for a while in my head, I thought, did not mess up with my schoolwork otherwise aunty Amara would have dropped me like a hot potato. Little did I know that she was bragging about how good, dedicated, and intelligent I was. What I considered to be a boring life of agony that revolved around sleep, eat, study, and sleep again turned out to be a life of diligence in the eyes of others. Well, my diligence paid off because I always took the first to the third position in my class. In my pain, I concluded I was a miserable, shy, and lonely child. But other people saw me as a virtuous young person. The quiet, serious way I carried myself portrayed me in my Igbo culture as a virtuous girl who did not live a carefree life.

In a sense, what I thought was bad for me turned around for my good. My Igbo culture expects young women to reserve themselves. I was not surprised when troops of young men seeking wives visited my home with their mothers or relatives to seek my hand in marriage whenever I was in my hometown during the vacation. In our compound at the time there were about four of us marriageable girls. Yet whenever I visited the village and a young man came for a future bride, he was looking for me. The first time it happened, an older woman had visited us with a young man whom she said was her nephew. I greeted our guests, but soon learned that the young man was interested in marrying me. The expression on my face was like "Wow, I do not want to get married now. I am still in school, and marriage is the last thing in my mind." The young man tried to convince me that he would very willingly allow me to complete school and pursue my desired academic career. As he offered me heaven and earth, I softly asked him his name. He replied that his name was Barnabas. Straining to make sure I heard him right, I asked again, and he replied, Barnabas.

"Hmmm, what do you do for a living?" He stated he was a Customs officer with fleets of houses and cars. I muttered "Hmm" again. The fact was that I had issues with both his profession and his name. I remembered how my classmates had had issues with my name, Amoris. It was a bad feeling. I shuddered as I wondered why any parent would give their child the name of a thief in the bible, an awful thief that people had chosen instead of Christ, their savior. I thought about his name Barnabas. Then I told him that I was still in school and that my aunty who was sponsoring my education did not lack the funds for my education. I added that I would not commit until I graduated from college. They left disappointed. But I was polite with them. I concluded that men like Barnabas would abuse their wives. His job as a custom officer disqualified him in my estimation. In Nigeria, it was alleged that custom officers were fraudulent, took bribes, cheated and stole from people. The community generally looked upon them as thieves. Evidently, the allegations must be true. Otherwise how could a young man of 25 like Barnabas boast of multiple cars and houses. His likes were for girls who wanted to marry riches. I was looking for someone to fill many vacuums in my life. Riches were at the bottom of my list of criteria of my prospective groom. Earlier, I had determined that my future husband must be educated. My argument had always been that rich people were often concerned about their money. They put their minds on their wealth and when that wealth disappears, they resort to drinking and abusing their wives. May God forbid! For the remainder of my stay in the village that season, once any woman entered my compound with a young man, and this happened numerous times, I already knew they were coming for me. So, from the backyard, I would watch them enter our living room, and then I would jump through the window and disappear. I did this to avoid answering the questions of whether I would marry them or not.

The trend of events in my life at that time gradually led me to change my theology that I was this rejected and abandoned loner. I began to gain some confidence in life. I was operating under the high expectation placed on me by my aunty, Amara. On one occasion, I witnessed her place a bet with my uncle Jide, her husband. She betted with him that I would come straight home after my lectures and would not branch off to any other place. Uncle Jide, an American from a different culture, did not agree with her that a girl my age had no other interests besides school. I believe she told him to put his money where his mouth belonged, and he did. When I came back as my aunty had boldly assured Uncle Jide, her husband, I saw her thrust out her hand to my uncle, who promptly handed her the money they had agreed on. For me, this incident was super trustworthy. Though the pressure to excel was high, I was happy that it was for a good cause.

I also noticed that Uncle Ejike was fighting to take me away from Aunt Amara, his sister. I have heard it said that life was like a box of chocolate. You never knew what you would get each time. Here was I, Amoris, the once rejected and abandoned child, I have now become the sought-after by suitors and relatives who were showing up to claim her. All I knew was that my aunt inherited me. I could see that my aunty enjoyed making her older brother mad whenever they engaged in their sibling disputes. She often threw it in his face that she was the only capable person their mother could entrust to inherit Amoris. That was why she had inherited me from Mama. I also guessed that my uncle saw how my auntie Amara was so proud of my accomplishments. So, whenever he wanted to tease aunty Amara, he would do things for me.

One day, he made the mistake of openly bragging in my presence that he would take me from my aunt because she was a woman and he should have inherited me not she. I was angry and heartbroken because I was then at the point when I was settling down to a peaceful life of gratitude. I could not understand why he was opening old wounds for me. I was so broken into pieces and angry with my uncle that I began to weep bitter tears again. In my tears, I respectfully asked him where he was before that time. I asked him to explain why he found it appropriate to come now to cart me away like a piece of furniture. He was startled, for he never thought I could challenge him with such questions. His fight with my auntie gave me a chance to tell him to his face that he could not inherit me since I was not up to being inherited. My confrontation put the matter to rest forever.

Chapter 11

Meeting and Marrying Mr. Right

My final year at the university became more intense because I became the girl behind the mask. I still consistently maintained my life of isolation hidden behind the mask of round-the-clock attention to my studies. I would stand by the library door waiting for it to open, and once it opened, I entered and marched straight to my choice seat. I studied till the library closed then I went back to my hostel to sleep only to wake up again to the same routine. Most of the time, I encountered young men at the library, trying to get my attention either for friendship or marriage I guessed. My reactions indicated lack of interest and I guess this either intimidated or annoyed them. I usually dismissed each one before he could even come closer. My close-up life and steady habit made men misread my plight for pride. Unknown to me a group of five young men had vowed among themselves that one of them must get me. One of the five called Kemi, was a good friend of Nnamdi, a young man who worked under Aunty Amara at the same university. Kemi had informed Nnamdi that there was this chick at the Education library that proved tough to get. So, he and his friends had betted on who would get the Babe first. Kemi did not know Nnamdi was related to aunty Amara as a family and that she took him as a son. Kemi confirmed to Nnamdi that he was going to Ijebu Ode to get a charm he would use to get this young lady. Nnamdi asked Kemi why he did not approach the lady head-on and ask her for a date. Kemi confessed that he had been leaving love notes on her study cubicle but had sadly watched her fold the notes and toss them into the garbage bin. Nnamdi asked Kemi to show him this damsel that was giving them this much trouble. Kemi brought Nnamdi to the library, where he pointed Amoris out to Nnamdi.

"Kemi, are you sure this young lady you are pointing at is the one for whom you plan to go to Ijebu Ode to get charms?" Nnamdi asked Kemi.

"Yes!" Before Kemi knew what was happening, Nnamdi grabbed him by the neck to choke him.

He informed Kemi that Amoris was the daughter of Dr. Amara, his boss, who treated him as a son. Nnamdi added that he took that young lady as his own sister and had dedicated his life to protect her. Nnamdi held Kemi in that chokehold until Kemi begged and promised to get his competitors to keep off. I came to learn about this much later in life after I became Nnamdi's wife, though Nnamdi too had to prove himself worthy of my hand. More of that later in this narrative. But before marriage, I continued with my studies thanking God that my life was now filled with less trauma and more peace. I completed my exams with flying colors.

Sometimes, I wondered about those young men who left love notes on the desk where I studied in the library. I chuckled at the speed at which I yanked off and tore the notes to pieces. I didn't even mind if those who placed the notes were right there watching to see how I responded to their messages. I made sure that I did not read the notes. I must confess that thinking about this experience of my life now gave me a feeling of gratitude that I, Amoris, was loved and sought after by peers. This realization gave me hope and strengthened my determination to succeed. I think I had misinterpreted some of the happenings around me then because I was driving myself to a breaking point to uphold the remarkably high expectations of my auntie. The anxiety that I might lose my home was ever present. I stayed on and graduated with an excellent result.

Now my life revolved around a new horizon and a new phase. I believe that God was watching over me and protecting me. I learned from the Word of God that when you believe in God's will, he breaks every protocol for you. I learned that those who fear God lack nothing, if only they exercise patience. We will recall that because Joseph prevailed in all his trials and hardships, he went from the pit into which the brothers had thrown him to Potiphar's house as a slave. From there, he went to prison for a crime he did not commit before he got promoted to the second highest position in the land of Egypt. In addition, he received the rights of the firstborn child from Jacob, his father, who gave his two sons equal inheritance with the other tribes of Judah. I want you to know that there is no temptation that you are passing through that someone else has not experienced. There are times for tests and trials. At such times if we do not allow the devil to derail us we will receive God's promise of his word that says, "Ask God of anything in the name of Jesus, he will do it for you." I built trust in the Lord when I was studying for my exams. God came through for me and I passed my exams satisfactorily. I lived a life of gratefulness and assurance. Now, before I take any test, I fast and pray. While I prepared for that exam, I usually tell God what grade I wanted to receive, and I always got exactly that grade. I get expected results through prayer and fasting.

Among my people after a young woman graduates from post-high school, she is expected to get married and make a home with her husband, if she considers herself a responsible young woman. Earlier, I explained that many men were coming to ask for my hand in marriage. I finally narrowed the list down according to my expectations. I did not want rich or flamboyant men. I prayed to God to give me someone with whom I would build my married life. I had this notion that already-made men treated their wives as possessions or property to be added to their collection. I believed that if they ceased to be wealthy, they would abuse their wives. Again, everything I did was centered on what I was going through. The most important desire of mine was to have someone whom I would call my own. For me, a husband meant security. My husband should give me security and that would be the greatest pleasure of my life. Since my life had been controlled at different times by my auntie, my grandmother and since I never had a sister or brother or even father, I prayed to God to give me that one person that would fill all these voids in my life. It did not matter that at the time I was musing and praying for such an individual, I would not talk to anyone, let alone speak to suitors. One could aptly describe me as a woman who believed that all men abused and abandoned their wives. I could be regarded as a young woman who hated men because at that time in my life, I blamed men for the trials and predicaments of my life. This emotional state may explain why I was never curious or determined to seek out my father and find out how he looked. I never even asked my sister who told me about his existence to show me his picture or take me to meet him.

My grandmother had often emphasized the serious issues that surrounded male-female relationships. If men touched me, I would be pregnant. At my young age, I took her words literally. If a man placed his hand on any part of my body, no matter which part, I would instantly get pregnant. Yes, I mean it and please excuse my naivety for taking that statement literally when I did. Remember, I did not have peers who would debunk my understanding of some of my grandmother's teachings. I thoroughly internalized what I heard from my grandmother despite my exposure to university education. I did not have a boyfriend nor desired one. I had gathered much confidence from the fact that men were flocking our home to marry me. I also had built-in strength from the knowledge that my auntie trusted me and was proud of me.

At the height of this season of my life, I decided to find that special man by myself. I declared a 7-day fasting and praying as I had learned from my grandmother. I asked God to bring me my husband at the end of my fast. At the conclusion of the fast, I identified and narrowed my prospective suitors to four young men who had been working with my family in one capacity or the other, though none of their positions of work had anything to do with me. As far as I could remember, any young man who came closer to me became an automatic enemy. I suspected that they were trying to touch me and get me pregnant. The first guy, Livinus, went indirectly through my extended family in the village. He had studied engineering and was a wizard in Mathematics. He connected himself with me by assisting me with some of my Math course assignments. When I was not there, he visited my family members in the village, helped them with errands. He had informed them of his long-term interest in me and so had endeared himself to the family. Still, I had my reservations. One day he formally proposed to me. I assessed him mentally. I wanted my future mother-in-law to love me as her daughter and fill the void I had as a motherless girl. My marital package also included a father-in-law who would be the father I never had. But Livinus had lost his father. To compound issues, the day he introduced me to his mother, she had looked me up and down, and her body language spelt disapproval in highlighted, bold, block letters. I may not have said much in those days, but I read people very well; I assimilated and decoded events around me powerfully. I crossed her son's name off the radar for good. The three others, Matthew a teacher, Ossy, an accountant and Nnamdi, a computer programmer, all met my requirements, but I could not marry all three. The process of elimination then set in.

The man, who eventually won my heart, had a distinguishing factor in his favor. He had a tough time getting to me, but he scaled the hurdles without stumbling, a factor that assured me that my future husband had arrived. You will recall the young man, Nnamdi, who worked in my aunt's office when I was studying Math at the university. This was the same young man God used to stop the men who had set a bet to use charm on me. Yes, Nnamdi always came to our home to carry out errands for my aunt, his boss. I looked up to him as an older brother. And he was my older brother in a way because my aunt treated him like a son. Whenever he was in our house, like a big brother, he helped me in my chores and shopping. If I needed school supplies, my auntie sent him to the stores. I felt very safe and secure with him; he cared for me as if I was his younger sister. I felt so secure around him that I often visited his residence and played tennis with his friends. I derived great joy when I beat them at that game because tennis was the only sport I enjoyed and played well. He had a close friend named Okey, who often hung out with him. I was secure with Nnamdi for he had his own girlfriend that visited him at the time. It was my self-appointed role to check out any girl and give approval for the go-ahead. He often took pictures of me and my niece, my aunt's only child, Cynthia. Unknown to me, he shared these pictures of my niece and me with his mother in the village. On one of his visits to his village, his mother woke him up early to have a serious talk with him. She pleaded with him not to refuse her request. He promised his mother that if it was something he could do; he would do it and she did not need to wake him up in the middle of the night to make her request. The older woman then dug into her blouse and pulled out my picture. She begged him to go bring the young woman in that picture to her as a daughter-in-law. Nnamdi recounted that he nearly wetted his pants. It was not as easy as his mother had imagined it. How on earth could he go to his boss and ask for her daughter's hand in marriage? Incidentally, he had gone to the village expressly to see a young woman his father had recommended for him for a future partner. And here was his mother raising an impossible obstacle that should not be there, in his view. To compound the matter, the two families came from two different parts of Igbo land who spoke different dialects of Igbo language. He recovered the picture from his mother without promising her anything. When he got back to the city, he prayed over the picture of the woman whom he had taken as a baby sister until his mother planted this crazy idea in his mind. Nnamdi related his experience to his best friend, Okey. Okey was quick to encourage him to make a proposal first.

The day Nnamdi first proposed to me, the three of us had gone out together. Then, Nnamdi requested a private discussion with me. I was nervous and worried at the same time. He assured me not to worry at all. Then, he said;

"Amoris, I will love you to be my wife." In an instant, I saw my entire world crashing down. He wanted to know what I thought of what he had just said. I searched for an answer but found none. When I found words, they were,

"Over my dead body." Then I ran home like someone who had seen a ghost. For a full one year I avoided Nnamdi whenever he came to our house because he worked in my aunt's office. If he visited, I would go into my room and not come out until he left. Of course, he knew I was in the house. He found a way to make me know he knew I was hiding from him. He would often shout on his way out,

"Madam Amara, Amoris, I am leaving." One day he screamed "Madam Amara, Amoris, I am going" but he did not leave. He had hidden next to my room and when I came out of my hideout, Nnamdi ran to me, grabbed me and landed a hot passionate kiss on my cheek. Then, he said to me,

"I must marry you." The certainty in his voice was compelling. He smiled and left. I was so furious that I started crying. Why would my brother whom I trusted so much betray my trust and desire to marry me? Each time, I deliberated on the possibilities of him being my husband; I shivered with confusion and anger. Although I had no relationship with my biological brother from my mother, I refused to accept that Nnamdi was not my brother in the real sense. It was his work relationship with Aunty Amara, his boss that brought us to know one another and treat each other as siblings. I resorted to another session of 7-day prayer and fasting as Mama Nnukwu had taught me.

On the 7th[th] day of my self-declared fasting and prayer, I specifically asked God to reveal my husband to me. I thanked God for always honoring my prayer. After that prayer, I got up, opened the door of my room to go use the restroom, which was outback. As I opened my door, I saw Nnamdi, at my door, completely dressed in his National Youth Corps Service (NYSC) uniform. His right hand was raised to knock at my door. We both stood there speechless. I stood there open-mouthed wondering what had just happened. This could only be a miracle! What amazing and speedy answer to my prayer! This same Nnamdi whom I said I would marry over my dead body was standing at my door as answer to my prayer. He was in shock as well and transfixed for a moment. When he eventually spoke, he said

"Madam, your aunt, had sent me to collect your nephew's transfer certificate from you." I gave him the document and then he requested me to accompany him to meet his mother who desired to see me. I said,

"Yes, I will go with you?" He was not sure I had heard his request, so he repeated it. I repeated my response,

"Yes, I will go with *you* to meet *your* mother in *your* village." I clearly saw God's hand in choosing a husband for me. Nnamdi could not understand my sudden change of position.

We journeyed to his village the same day. On getting to his family, a series of miracles happened. His siblings: five sisters and three brothers ran out of the main house, screaming happily, Dedenne, meaning "Our big brother is back." Yet, each ran past him and ran to me and hugged me as if they had known me for years. They had not known that we were visiting home that day. When we got inside the house, Nnamdi held my hand, walked me towards his mother and handed me to her with these words,

"Mama, this is Amoris whom you asked me to bring to you."

His mother broke down crying. While she was crying, she hung unto me and rained hot tears on me. I held tightly to her as well. I thought that I understood the smile of victory on her face amid her tears. When she stopped crying, she called me the name Chinyere meaning "God has given." Soon, his father returned. When he saw me, he embraced me and gave me the name of Chikaodili, meaning "It all depends on God." It appeared that my visit was more exciting to Nnamdi's father. The next day, he took me on a ride on his motorcycle. He rode around the entire village showing me off to everyone in the community. The reception that Nnamdi's' family gave me was so definitive that he did not need to propose to me again. After that visit, I was proclaimed his wife by his family. Nnamdi's only problem currently was how to tell my aunt of his intentions. My feelings gradually shifted from seeing him as my brother and I accepted him and agreed to be his wife. He finally asked my aunt for my hand in marriage and my aunt surprised us with her immediate approval. She assured us that she knew all along that he was interested in me. She gave her blessings and we became husband and wife.

With my marriage to Nnamdi, I found trust, real love and friendship. I found a new home that was exclusively mine and a new family that loved me very much. I felt so blessed that God had packaged all I ever dreamed of and handed it all to me in one package. I had a father-in-law that accepted me like his own, a mother-in-law, and siblings-in-law that suffocated me with the kind of love seen only in movies. I made a silent vow to God that I would cherish the husband that he had given me. I am often reminded that I was not blessed unless I became a blessing to others. Consequently, I prayed to God to empower me in such a way that I would be able someday to give back to others.

Chapter 12

Moved to a foreign land

Married life exposed me to different seasons and different forms of fulfillment. My heart experienced testament to its desires. I journeyed through the bliss of heaven in gradual elevation up a hill happily. I was determined to actualize that Promise Land of ever after. But disaster and pain seemed to always locate me. Now, I had a very loving husband; my husband loved me more than life itself and through him, I had my own four children, a father-in-law and mother-in-law who loved me so much that they took me as their own. At first, I did not know how to joggle this knowledge or the concomitant feelings. I was overwhelmed by so many positive emotions that I tried to eliminate some of the drama. I wondered if all these good things happening to me at the same time could be for good.

In many African traditions, you do not give tragic news to women and children directly. News of the death in any family goes first to the eldest male member of the family or kindred. That elder then calls other men in the family and tells them what has happened before they inform the women and the children. This chain of delivering tragic news to a family member is followed no matter how close the victim of the tragedy is to the recipient of the tragic news. You will recall that my aunt failed to give me any information about my mother. But she promptly and privately related the story of my background to my husband, Nnamdi, to the point of giving him details of my mother Amelia and her life story. She made Nnamdi promise that he would protect my life with his last breath. Stressing that I was an offspring of an abusive father, she admonished him to ensure that I never experienced abuse in our relationship. Nnamdi, my husband, promised her that he would never abuse me. He kept his promise.

What an irony! For years I had been seeking answers to the critical question of who I was but got no answers. Yet, as soon as I got married, my aunt spilled the entire information to a newly acquired family member. I think that this tradition which hides the truth from the right person, just to protect the person, often achieves the opposite effect. An adverse effect of this tradition that has to be explored and eradicated is that often, people who encountered the situations in their lives where vital information was withheld from them because they were young often swore never to repeat the same mistakes. But, somehow, they subconsciously repeat the same. After she was widowed, Amoris recalled with shock that she had withheld vital information from her own children, expressly because she wanted to spare them emotional upheaval. She and her husband had withheld Nnamdi's serious medical condition from their children with the fear that their children's academic programs would be compromised if they knew of their father's serious sickness. Amoris later learned from each of her children, that they wished they had known of his condition while he was alive. The children explained to her that the trauma and struggles they faced after his death was more disastrous than the protection their parents' decision set out to provide to them. Amoris concludes that, many times people who experienced peculiar obstacles in life often repeat a cycle of the same trauma they overcame later in their life. I sincerely warn against this cultural trait.

Nnamdi and I wedded in Nigeria, but we moved to the United States where Nnamdi had secured a good job. As expected, life in the US was brand new to me. The food, dressing, jobs, children's behaviors, adult behavior towards others, the culture, in general, was different, and relationships were out of this world experiences. Still, I joyfully scaled through it all determined to survive and thrive in this foreign land. My husband and I complained a lot about the differences. It was normal for couples to argue and I recall our very first argument. It centered on me taking my vitamins. He had tried to make me take my vitamins because of the cold weather. He argued that I needed them to boost my immune system. He did not know that I usually thrashed the vitamins he gave me. I had just joined him in the US and was not used to vitamins. One day, I wanted to know why he was drugging me when I was not ill. In Nigeria, we called medications drugs and you only took them when you were ill. I did not know any better. Nnamdi could not believe what he was hearing. Dumbfounded, he sat me down for a heart-to-heart talk.

It was after one significant disagreement about vitamins that Nnamdi, my husband, broke into tears. He quietly and calmly narrated details of my background as given to him by my aunt, whom we had left behind in Nigeria. He had details about my mother, Amelia, and her death in a foreign land and reiterated his promise to my aunty to protect me with his life. Now, I was gathering bits and pieces of what happened to my late mother from my husband. Wow, so much was coming out about me from my husband after a marital disagreement. The vital information I had sought all my life was being released to me at the wrong time and place, in the wrong manner, and by the wrong person. I could not handle it. I was bitter that my husband was the one giving me these details of my mother's life and death. I doubted the story; I even doubted his motives for telling me in the first place. How was I to know that he was not tilting the story to suit himself?

My husband however, diligently kept his promise to my Aunty Amara to protect me with his life. None of his family members could talk to me without going through him first. In my culture, in-laws blamed the wife for anything that went wrong in the marriage or with the man. His family could not do that in my case, because Nnamdi put his life on the line for anything concerning me. It appeared that with that promise to my aunt, Nnamdi had secretly pledged his life in exchange for mine. He lived his life as if keeping me alive was his divine assignment. On my side, I wanted him to be alive and safe; those two conditions, his life and his safety, completed my own life. My own experiences led me to swear that my own children would have the knowledge of anything that legitimately concerned their lives. I even got them to learn to swim as a deterrent to my near-drowning episode during the civil war. The shadows of my past had a frustrating way of showing up around me. They showed up in my child rearing skills, in every task I performed. I anxiously swore to provide for children in my life all that I lacked, do everything for them. I tried to feed them to death. Now, they have learned not to tell me any food they liked because I would flood the house with that food. I provided everything I thought they wanted. Many times, I was wrong until it dawned on me that I was trying to satisfy my own unfulfilled needs and not my children's present needs.

I developed a passion for helping children and I provided for the children around me with love, compassion, and respect. I searched for jobs that involve helping children. I accepted and did jobs that enabled me to serve children in need. I gave them all assistance as much as I had the capacity regardless of the difficulty and challenges that I encountered along the way.

Next, I got a cleaning job with McDonalds. I already held a bachelor's degree, but I could not find a suitable job because I was a foreigner in a foreign land. That cleaning job was tough. Although I met kids there, I could not reach them, so I quit the job. My next job was that of a mail carrier. I accepted the position because that was what I could get, and I needed an income. I did not last long in this position too because the tasks were highly challenging even though the pay was good. After my stint there I developed a high respect for post office mail carriers. That position taught me discipline, punctuality, and diligence no matter the weather conditions. But I could not handle it, so I quit. The long-winding journey in search of my desired position eventually brought me to the classroom to teach children. I was now at my destination, or so I thought.

My first day in class was memorable. As soon as the children came into class, one child stood up and asked me, "Who is this Kunta Kinte?"

"From which ship did this one land?" The entire class erupted into laughter. The children laughed hard and long, but I comported myself and allowed them to go on for a while. Then I calmly asked them if they were done. I informed them firmly that I was their teacher and had come to stay. I further made it clear that the behavior they had exhibited was not tolerated in my class. Surprisingly, those students and I got on very well to our mutual benefit. As if the behavior of the children was not enough culture shock, one day a white female staff member in the building asked me how I came to the United States. She asked the question in a smock tone that gave her away? I told her,

"Oh, I hopped from tree to tree like a monkey until I got here, and it took me many days. She immediately apologized and tried to make it sound good. I assured her not to worry. Who was going to tell her that the encounter with her was nothing compared to what I had been through in my life? I had specialized in surviving strange situations. I made up my mind that the field of teaching presented a need that I could fill. So, I settled on teaching children, but I also got a job as a child protective service worker. I did both jobs concurrently.

While I was a child protective service social worker, I encountered the case of a two-year old girl who had been sexually abused. When I got to the hospital to investigate the matter, the attending physician informed me that the little girl was sexually abused. The little girl had been brought in as a result of high fever. On examination, they found her private part oozing with puss and smelling horribly. A sex abuse exam was consequently performed. Further investigation revealed that her mother was a drug user and whenever she wanted a fix, the men demanded sex in return. But they would not desire sex from her; rather, they wanted a fresher body since hers was already too contaminated by her drug use. This drug-abuser mother then offered her two-year old to those drug-infested men. That was how the girl came to her predicament. I could only imagine the degree of trauma that child would have as she grew up and how her life would turn out later. Accordingly, I removed the child and went to court to make sure the child received justice.

Throughout this ordeal, I was a walking dead since I had never seen anything like that in my entire life. I could not imagine in a million years that anything like that existed. I remained at this job because I needed a job and I had a deep emotional attachment to children's burdens. I convinced myself that I was created to save the world's children, no matter the emotional baggage involved nor its weight on me. This case of sex abuse contributed to the anxieties I felt with people around my two growing daughters. Just like the trauma I went through after I experienced the near drowning experience led me to enroll all four in swimming classes at an early age of six years. For the children, swimming was fun, but for me, I swore that all my children must know how to swim. I was still a child protection service staff when The World Trade Center was attacked. This incident transported me back to my days of loneliness while living with my grandmother. I could see the children I encountered living lives of hopelessness, helplessness and loneliness. I saw my life through every child who lost parents in that dreadful World Trade Center terrorist attack. It seemed to me that fate connived with the attack to put my life on the emotional replay button. As child protection services, my agency staff were often first responders. Assigned workers shuttled nonstop for months taking care of children who lost their parents during that attack. My colleagues performed their tasks because the position demanded that they did what they were doing. I made countless visits to the hospital with a traumatized child whose parents could not be located; I made frantic searches through the list of the deceased at the World Trade Center site on forty-second street New York City wishing for the inevitable. I immersed myself in continuous prayer as I searched for the parents of the child I had just visited at the hospital, whose horror-stricken eyes stuck in my head and whose fearful face was familiar. For me, I walked in the same shoes as those children who would never meet their parents again. I watched some of them end up with grandparents as I did some with other family members and very few ended up in foster care. I dreaded the thought that those children would experience the life of orphans like I did. Every day of the months I worked nonstop with this population, I wept day and night because I concluded that life was hopeless. Surprisingly, I remained at this job for 11 years before I settled exclusively in the teaching job. I knew that I always wanted to give back to children.

While teaching, I looked out for my students and I had the rare skill of identifying children who needed care and love. Once I identified their needs, I extended myself to fill those needs. I became that grandmother teacher who always had snacks for the needy child. With time, my students knew where to go for what they needed. I counseled them to persist no matter what challenges they experienced. I usually paid special attention to all the students raised by their grandmothers and I shared my life stories with them. Lunchtime became a haven for some of them. There was this one boy, Bertine, whom I sat down and shared my experiences as a child raised by my grandmother. I confessed to him that I cherished my grandmother very much for what she had done for me. I shared details of my difficulties and fears as a young person growing up with my grandmother, and I vowed that I would never do anything to bring her pain. After I shared my story with him, the young man, Bertine, was heartbroken; tears streamed down his face as he promised to appreciate his grandmother better. From then on, if he did something wrong at home, his grandmother would call me and request me to speak to him and encourage him to return straight home and on time. There was this one-time, Bertine, had gone out with friends and they had dented someone's car. Bertine was caught and grandmother had to pay for the damages. She called me again and I spoke to the young man and made him realize the difficulties to which he was exposing his grandmother. I was the one who imposed a curfew on him. He was not to be out after 10pm. This way, he would not get into trouble. He observed the curfew and he always checked in with me whenever he got to school.

As a teacher I met another student who was being raised by his grandmother. I quickly recognized peculiar mannerisms and characteristics of my youthful years. In class, he was always quiet and diligent with his work. He was one of the students who privately visited my classroom at lunch time to discuss their difficulties and needs. I was always available to listen and direct him. I also confidently shared my story with him. He recounted how he had been moved very often until he was separated from his grandmother whom he had grown to love and cherish. She had gotten into some problems with the law and the Division of Youth and Family Services (DYFS) came to move him again. He confessed to me that he ran away from the group home they placed him in and currently lived in an abandoned building from where he came to school daily. He did not want to be moved again into another home. I was devastated and told him to always come for supplies like food, clean clothes, and occasionally, money for laundry. I provided him these supplies till he left the school. I continued to encourage him to believe that God will bless and direct the rest of his destiny. So, through the jobs I did, I saw things differently. Life challenges became stranger, and the road appeared more rugged.

Chapter 13

Life into Widowhood

Regardless of all ills and sharp turns in relationships, my husband and I shared a love-filled life. I respected him highly, and he likewise did the same for me. God blessed us with four gorgeous children, two boys, and two girls whom we raised in a God-fearing environment. My husband loved the Lord with much passion. His life centered on priests and the religious. He invited multiple priests and nuns to our home and made them his brothers and sisters.

Broken, but not Beaten, is now taking a different but dramatic turn. As I relaxed in my new and settled lifestyle, confident that all was now well with me, turbulence struck after 25 many years of a happy, loving, married life? First, my husband got into an auto accident where he hit his head on the windshield of his car. He informed me that he had gotten into an accident but that he was fine. Little did he know that he had punctured his eardrum. That same night he had liquid gushing out of his ears. I rushed him to the hospital. There, the physicians diagnosed him with high blood pressure and diabetes. His health deteriorated from then on, and my life changed drastically. My husband died! Tragedy had struck me, Amoris again, this time very deeply? At first, I thought I was dreaming. I reasoned,

"No, God will not allow my husband to die knowing where I had been and how I got here to have him in my life." The only breath of fresh air I had was snuffed out in a twinkle of an eye. I countered the thought, "It is not true. This is hopeless." "This was a false apparition and movie that would soon stop." I tried to stop the dream but to no avail. I asked God these questions: "Must anyone who comes close to loving me die? Must anyone I depend upon and love with my heart die? I decided that I would not allow my children to love me anymore so that they would not be next. I blacked in and out for days, darkness fell over me. I looked ahead in a daze but saw nothing. The only man who brought meaning and stability into my life was dead. After two days in the darkness, I urged myself to stay up and break out of this dream, convincing myself that my husband was still alive and well. When finally, I came to and was now conscious to fully be aware of what had happened: that my husband, Nnamdi, was dead, that my only confidant, my only covering, the only human that assured me that I was truly a real person was dead. I had no choice but to accept it.

I went through my husband's burial silently from then on, and I fell into a seemingly bottomless pit of brokenness. A year later, while I was still in a state of depression, I attended his memorial service. Among my people, a widow mourned her husband for twelve months wearing all black. She remained indoors, going nowhere or attending no social activities. These sacrifices she was required to make to honor her husband's memory. In my situation, I extended the mourning period. I removed and burned the mourning clothes as tradition demanded. But I continued to shut myself away from people and social activities.

To make matters worse, a close friend, closer than a sister, my confidant, a lady who would defend me anywhere - be it a physical fight or other, she was firm in the forefront of my defense. She took no garbage from anyone. She had helped me in all kinds of difficulties. Our children grew up together and we helped each other with childcare challenges, food sharing and otherwise. Within one year of losing my husband, this sister I had discovered in the United States of America went to bed one night but did not wake up the next morning. It is said that sometimes when trouble comes as it rains but it pours. I feared that the only thing around me was death. I started deliberating on what could be the cause of all this death around me. In my thought process, I remembered that the bible says that God is jealous. That means, He will not share what belongs to him with anybody else. I convinced myself that I belonged to God and was not supposed to belong to anybody else. I knew that this revelation would be bad news for my children. They were already protecting me like an egg. I decided to end these mysteries. On January 16, 2016, I donated myself to God and changed my name to "Amoris of Jesus" from that day. I began to weed everything that I used to love or to which I had attached myself out of my life. My children were all confused and worried because of my moodiness and lack of desire to live on. One day they called a meeting, where all four agreed to call me to order. They convinced me that they themselves were a great reason to live on. In truth, they were out to help me overcome my darkness. But their attempt to help addressed the wrong reason for my affliction at that time. To me I was weeding everyone out so that they do not die. To my children, they recognized that they had to do whatever it took to save the only parent they had left. The irony of it all was that while I was in a bad shape, help was coming from my children, but I was too blind to notice. I began to hate nursing, hospitals, and everything connected to the hospital. I thought that if my mom did not study nursing in England, maybe she would be alive today.

After these deaths, I fell deep down into a pit of hopelessness again. Ironically, I seemed to be comfortable in my depression. My life centered on work, eat, pray, and sleep. Anywhere people gathered to pray, I was there. I joined a prayer family that read the bible online and prayed together as well. It was through daily logging on to this online prayer group, that God kept me sane. My life revolved around what the prayer group was doing, be it women retreat, fasting and praying for family needs, mission trips to different countries, I participated. I visited Israel during my life in the desert and had an experience of doing mission work in Israel, where my group fed the homeless. Each homeless individual ministered to me with their dilemma. In the end, a successful life is not about the inevitable brokenness that afflicts it but the burning desire in refusing to be beaten.

Chapter 14

Transformation into a Life of Praise

I came to understand the preaching of the word of God to a human person in the context that people should be careful not to worship another god for when anyone loves anything more than God that thing you love more than God has become your idol. When we lack a thing in our life, we tend to put our entire drive in gaining that thing lacking in our life; sometimes, that pursuit becomes an idol in our life.

Many people do not have stable homes like me that when we got one, our home became our idol. People get obsessed with one thing or the other and that becomes one's idol. Some people are prisoners to food; in this case, food is their idol. Some love their cars, and some love their jobs that they go to work to the point of neglecting their families and everything else; or they love their spouse to death, or their children are above everything else. All these idols are from past broken life experiences.

The Bible said that once any lifestyle has become someone's idol, it becomes unacceptable to God. I learned this from the Bible studies that I immersed myself in. Once I offered myself to God, I have to know what he wants from me. I told my tribe members to call me Amoris of Jesus, which they did. I also had a chance to be among a panel of women that testified on their life experiences at a women's conference in Sandy Cove, MD in 2018. I had hoped my testimony would help others draw strength from my experiences. it was then that I narrowed down all the turmoil going on in my life. I discovered that I was in training, and I began to persist and started restructuring my ideas. What is God training me to learn from all these tragedies? What is my life purpose? I determined that I must find and serve in that purpose for which God created me on earth.

I started analyzing my peculiar destiny; I told myself that God will not preserve my life all this time while through thick and thin for nothing. I recounted with understanding how God structured my path supernaturally from elementary school to graduate-level education, succeeding every step of the way. Once I pray and ask God specifically for whatever I want, I will get what I asked for. At this time, I reverenced God and said this was not just a common occurrence; it must be God working. I believe that I have a good gift of service to humanity. So I decided that since the Lord empowered me with the life of service, I will passionately serve children and my community with uncommon love and abandonment. I believed that in all situations, I find myself yearning for God's guidance that conquers all.

I cannot say that I transitioned into my new life that easily. I described in earlier chapters how I diligently joined a Bible school connected with a group of people that read the Bible from cover to cover every year. Most of the teachings I learned was from the daily reading and exaltation teachings. While I was still with the Bible reading group two years down the line, I met one of my children, *Godmother*.

The Lord used this lady who approached me and asked me if I will go with her to a Life in the Spirit Seminar offered at a Catholic Charismatic worship community that she belonged to and have been attending for a long time. I said yes, I would go with her. She was in shock, for her family has approached my husband and me and extended multiple invitations to us for the past ten years to join that God-worshipping community. We always declined their invitation with one excuse or the other. When I accepted that invitation and went to the seminar, I was reborn into a new life of praise and worship. I was renamed again with the name *Happy*, and at the end of the three-day seminar, I found a new peace that I never knew existed.

The process of the seminar encounter is that one is assigned a shepherd who will guide and train the lamb. God predestined a perfect shepherd for me. My transformation started with my shepherd, a destiny helper from heaven whom I believed was God's design for me. Tita Adel was away in the Philippines on a medical mission, but on the same night she came. She got a notice that she has to shepherd someone again, for she is the best one that can help me with my peculiar situations.

She took up that responsibility with a passion and love that I never imagined anyone had in them. With her guidance, I discovered my deep-rooted anger and unforgiveness. She guided me through getting them out of my system and freeing myself from the chains that bound me for years. She taught everything to me in a practical way. I began to trust and love again through the contagious, practical, deep love exemplar experience provided by my shepherd taught to me in that seminar.

My most significant transformation occurred through the lessons I learned from watching her and sharing with her. I found this peace and love that is pure; Tita Adel felt every pain, and I never hesitated to share my concerns and confusion with her. Gradually, I started letting go of my shadows and hidden fears. I avoided anyone caring about me for doubting that something wrong usually happens to them once transformed. I cautioned myself never to think like that again.

During the time I was under that confusing illusion, I carefully cut myself off from my best friend's family, my children, and even my shepherd, making sure that I stay away from them for fear of not letting anything happen to any of them.

I thank God that I found new peace with my newfound community. I learned how to praise God with complete abandonment. All the people I encountered there serve the

Lord with all their lives. I experienced disciples of God with a difference: they serve with happiness, and all their faces were glowing like those of angels. I was in awe and amazement that there are still saints serving God here on earth. Worshiping with that community, I learned how to praise my way out of any situation that I find myself in.

I shared my life contrition message from the perspective of praising God; on how God used all my brokenness to build me up and make me whom God wants me to be. I praised God for turning around all deaths of my loved family members for my good. The loss of my mother, grandmother, husband, and sister, and the lack of a father, trauma from war, domestic violence, and unstable home prepared me. I walked into a life of service to humanity and a life of gratitude for it was when I started praising God that he showered his grace in my life. I began to praise God for always providing a destiny helper for whatever lack that existed in my life.

It was only through the mercy of God that I had a super supportive husband, four highly achieving children in different fields and jobs, a home, and an excellent teaching career – all that I came to appreciate. I knew that I had crossed over, and I have landed into praise and thanksgiving. There is no turning back; the peace that I feel is unchangeable.

It was what led me to discover myself and discern my life's purpose. I came to the realization and believed that regardless of all life challenges, a person who goes through a transformational phase must not have any fear of the unknown. One must know that life's problems will only make one stronger because there is no champion without a context. The beautiful journey of today can only begin when we learn to let go of yesterday. I will say that for transformation to occur, one must put a padlock on the issues of yesterday and allow God to lead you to the future.

I learned a life of praise through knowing that when one encounters tremendous challenges, we have to trust God for his promise, and God will change your situation. Always remain humble, eradicate pride and envy, embrace the forgiveness of all people, and do not let the love of money direct your life ultimately, for so long as you soak yourself in the blood of the lamb and the word of God he will protect you till the end. At this point, I was singing God's praises, and I surrendered all my life's purpose into the hand of God. I said to God, I love you and ask you to send me wherever you want, for I will go, Lord, I will hold your people in my heart. Day in day out I listen to God's promises for God will fight all my battles, and I will keep my peace (Exodus 14:14).

I reminded God to contend with those that argue with me. I pray that God fights all my battles. I will hold my peace. This should be the only prayer that should be prayed by all reading this message. I believe that no matter what your situation is, if handed it God, consider it solved to hold your peace. My final thought will be through this life journey wherein Amoris found herself broken, but the blessing was that she triumphed. And So Can You.

Chapter 15: Broke out an Overcomer

The hero's people see every day are individuals like you and me. Oftentimes, heroes emerge instantly, at the spur of the moment. They are individuals who obey the first call for an act of faith and trust. The actions of most heroes are instant, spontaneous actions undertaken by individuals who give little or no thought to the consequences of those actions. I have observed that the moment people overcome their trials and transform into a new phase of life, they become a blessing to others when they share their adversities and the strategies, they had adopted to overcome the challenges they had faced. That is when such people become heroes. Heroes are Overcomers that are not afraid to act in faith and trust in the Supreme Being. When you challenge others to break out of their situation and not fear the unknown, you educate them that their limitations in life are because of their fear of the unknown. As you share and educate, you break people out of their mold and release an Overcomer.

Looking back, Mary, the mother of Christ Jesus, exhibited the first act of heroism. She displayed the deed of faith and trust. As soon as Angel Gabriel announced to her that she would be the mother of God, she immediately responded, "Let it happen to me, according to your word." Mary did not give any thought to what was coming to her, nor did she explore the consequences of such a decision. This makes her, in my view, the first hero ever. She exhibited the first act of faith and trust in God with complete abandonment. In our world today, acting in faith and complete trust in God with complete abandonment is a major characteristic of heroes.

You are a hero once you realize that you are not alone in a particular situation. You are a hero when you do whatever is needful to overcome your adversities. Responding and opposing what challenges face you without hesitation is an act of heroism. Whenever you exhibit faith in overcoming your trials, the creator of the universe steps out and carry you through with ease. Most heroes always look back at what they did and ask, "Did I do that?"

Broken but Not Beaten, So Can You, encourages its readers to praise their way out of difficulties by following these steps. Firstly, you must believe that you are fearfully and wonderfully made, and that God's works are perfect. Secondly, in every situation you find yourself you must give thanks to God. This is because he allows things to happen in your life for a reason. Thirdly, your breakout action gives you an opportunity to become fully aware of what is happening in your life, whether good or bad, and strengthen you to live through it faithfully. In the end, you can use the experiences as a ladder to change your life and your destiny. Fourthly, your greatness lies in your harnessing your God-endowed gift and talent by accepting the process, in letting go of past hurts, and in embracing your future with faith and trust. This breakout characteristic is exemplified in the life of America's latest and youngest hero and poet Amanda Gorman. This 22-year-old young lady captivated the whole world with her poem 'The Hill We Climb' recited at Joe Biden's (the oldest American President) Inauguration. Many might think of her appearance and performance at President Biden's inauguration as a coincidence. But I know it was preordained. Through young Amanda's persistence and passionate pursuit of her destiny despite the limitations and failures she encountered, she rose and acquired the prize of undeniable victory. My favorite nugget by Evangelist Joy Osueke Rolle says that

"Yesterday was your teacher; today is your testing, and tomorrow is your result. Life is a school with no time for trial and error." My takeaway from this nugget is that we must not allow ourselves to be beaten by our problems. We must sit up and kick down any comatose wall of routines we have repeatedly done and expected a different result.

Any time we exhibit the same behavior pattern it becomes habits that we regularly exercise with minimal to zero effort. This repetitive action keeps us in a comatose condition. After all, any action we routinely exhibit will yield an expected outcome. Amoris was broken but not beaten because in accepting what was coming to her with submission and faith in God, she harnessed that which God had planted in her. I believe that the key to everyone's happiness lies in blooming where God has planted one. What will make one great in life lies in discovering one's deep-rooted talent and diligently pursuing it alone.

We should always strive to discover the talent God has instilled in us. We should seek this talent out and pursue it. When we spend time idolizing other people's talent or even following others; talent, we fail or we find ourselves in a prolonged wilderness, a point of no return. Apostle Dr. Patience Oti in her teaching on Self -Esteem, explained that when we look in the mirror, whatever we see and tell ourselves we are, that is who we are. If we see ourselves as pretty, wonderfully made, and highly favored by God, that is who we are, and nothing changes that. But the opposite also is true. So, we must know who we are and hold on to that knowledge in everything we do no matter what threatens our lives at each stage of our existence. From that teaching, I gathered that those who isolate themselves promote self with undue relevance. They idolize or imitate others; they exhibit timidity and shyness; they give undue reverence to everyone. They are always critical and judgmental in addition to being very abusive. Such individuals have low self-esteem, and they take out their anger and insults on others around them.

Apostle Oti's teaching points out that excuses such as "I am weak," "I am too old," "I am too short, too tall, too young or even too ugly," or whatever excuse that is out there comes from low self-esteem. I am suggesting that for us to overcome our situation and break out of adversity we should drop all our fears, anxieties, excuses, and complaining.

We should rather act in faith and trust that we are not alone. With this determination, we never settle for less and we break out from any pit in which we might find ourselves. I also learnt from this and numerous other teachings of Apostle Patience Oti of the TRIBE Prayer line never to allow the wishes and opinions of the world about me to control me. To succeed in any sphere of life, one must learn the secret of those who succeeded before you in that area of life. Learning from such achievers, you seek out your talent and passionately pursue it till you succeed and encourage others to break out as I did.

We should not be discouraged when ignorant or envious people try to shut us down. We should learn to process every trial and use it as a ladder to climb out of our pit. We are blessed through the process of overcoming our trials. Amoris was glad that she found herself. She discovered the gift in her life that gave her the courage to live on. Once she made up her mind to live a life of gratitude by sharing the testimony of how God got her out of her broken life into a blessed life, she became an overcomer, gained her true-life freedom and elevated into new joyous life.

Dear reader, my final question to you will be; are you flourishing as a father, husband, mother, wife, daughter, son, friend, teacher, nurse, doctor, clergy, and an officer of the law, athlete, and citizen of your community? Are you busy drowning yourself in jealousy, hurt, complaining about a past hurt? Are you planning revenge due to unforgiveness of self and others, idolizing another person's success instead of seeking out and prospering in the gift God planted in you? As redirected, Amoris broke out of all her adversities without being beaten. She overcame all that life threw at her. Though she was "Broken" by the process, yet she was not "Beaten and So Can You."

Author's Remarks and Recommendations

Many times, broken men and women produced the most exceptional results ever recorded. It is the breaking of alabaster jar of oil in the bible that releases the sweet-smelling fragrance. Only a broken object needs fixing, naturally. Whatever presses you down on your knees is your oppressor. Whatever problem you have right now is your wilderness. Every life trial you face is what God wants to use to fix you so you can cross over to being a perfectly successful person ready to help others cross over. In *Broken but not Beaten*, Amoris tells her painful story of her life in the wilderness, yet through observing God's words and principles, she overcomes. The author testifies that amid trials, she praised her way out of whatever pit she found herself. It is important for you to unseat every oppressor in your life with praising and worshiping God. It was when Amoris, the lead character, studied and meditated on the Word of God that she heard the still small voice of God. That voice assured her that God would give her reasons for hope. God is God all by himself. He is no respecter of anyone. Every child God created is in

God's image and is unique and peculiar. All God's creation is uniquely made; tall, short, blond, white, black, green, or otherwise, each has a specific destiny. God seems to say,

"I know and call each of my creations by name before each is created. I always protect what I have ordained. I also confirm the calling in all my creation's life." Every one of God's creatures goes through specific training, which is to say, each experiences affliction through which God prepares his creations. Only those who persist and complete the due process receive the promise. Any life that derails from its due process misses the profit. While in training, patience becomes the only key for survival. God, who calls you, is a patient God. God's timing is all that counts. Your only passion is a determination not to die while in training. The worst tragedy anyone can ever face in life is to die without accomplishing the goal. "I am too old" or "I am too young," are unacceptable excuses. Neither should such other excuses about our height, color, eloquence, wealth, abilities stop you. Remember that God uses whomever he wants, whenever he wants, however he wants, and for whatever he wants to do. God's ways are not man's ways. God states that if the man he created in his image does not obey him, stones will. In my view, obedience to God remains the secret to one's success in life. Writing down your vision constantly reminds you to visualize it by believing and behaving it until you become it. The bible reminds us of Rachel, Jacobs' barren wife who had Joseph at God's time. We also remember Hannah, the barren woman who later bore Samuel, the prophet of God. David, the shepherd boy, was the youngest of his family. He had no kingly qualities in man's eyes, but he was anointed king by God. David went through years of persecution from the hands of Saul before he became king. King David's persecution was his training. His countless trials built his patience and humility, traits he needed to overcome the kingly challenges of his later life. God appears to be saying to all his creation,

"What shame do you think you bear that I have not seen?" "Have you read of my prophet, Hosea? I commanded him to go marry a prostitute and he did." No child I created should ever feel any shame. It does not matter whether you came out of date rape or other kinds of rape, whether your conception was planned or by mistake, whether you are abandoned or adopted you should feel no shame. Regardless of the circumstances that surround your birth, your existence on earth is of God's making. He alone knows his plans for your life. I advise you to seek and pursue God's plan for your life. For God that keeps you alive, knows his plans for you, and will always protect you.

From experience, I know that no condition is permanent in life, and patience is a virtue of God. God wants man to acquire patience as a gateway to prominence. I believe that those who acquire patience and humility overcome every stronghold of captivity. All oppression and attacks in their lives disappear with time.

Through the journey of writing this book I learned that love is never hopeless. From my prayer line, I learned that wisdom is the greatest wealth in life; I learned that the most potent weapon in life is patience. The best security system is faith, and the greatest medicine ever manufactured is laughter. The fascinating attribute of all these tools is that they are all free. It is in the bible that God's grace is without repentance. Whoever asks for it gets it free. God breaks protocol for anyone who asks, believes, trusts, and reaches out to take it. This book addresses issues that relate to all who have the mindset that events happening around them are hopeless. This book explores the options that show God's love hidden deep in all the trials one goes through. I have studied all the broken aspects of Amoris's life. Amoris found God's agape love in all those situations through which she went.

My favorite affirmations that I would like to share with readers all over the world include that everyone in the world is worth God's love. Jesus died for you and me, so we deserve to live. I am loved; I am still God's creation, and by his grace, I receive his compassion and salvation, so I am favored. As I rock my wilderness with praise and worship, my only question for you is, "Do you know who you are?"

You should not derail in your wilderness if you use the GPS (Global Positioning System). Be alerted to recalculate your way each time you think you have missed it. A good tip is to daily update your life to a new you, by using the Word of God; recalculate your way back without any fear despite mistakes you make, or relationships broken. Even loss of money, lives, jobs, or current sickness you may be facing, physical disability issues that attack your very existence will all turn out well if you GPS your way through with God's Word. If you have unforgiving deeds, if you suffered deep-rooted pain and abandonment, if you have lost home and school opportunities, recalculate a new you, and adapt to that new vision and responsibility in your life till you break out of whatever wilderness you are in. You will find out that once you get up and dust yourself, you should say to yourself, "I might be broken, but I am alive and standing. I am not alone. You will see that the divine purpose for your life will become yours.